Published by Pink Tree Publishing Limited in 2023

For questions and comments about this book, please contact
pinktreepublishing@gmail.com

www.pinktreepublishing.com
www.agathafrost.com

v 1.1

WANT TO BE KEPT UP TO DATE WITH AGATHA FROST RELEASES? *SIGN UP THE FREE NEWSLETTER!*

www.AgathaFrost.com

You can also follow **Agatha Frost** across social media. Search 'Agatha Frost' on:

Facebook
Twitter
Goodreads
Instagram

Other

CHAPTER ONE

*C*laire Harris hummed to the shop's radio as she arranged the last row of cured candles on the rustic circular display table. The soft spotlights cast a warm glow on the colourful jars, their bespoke foil labels glittering in neat rows. Her latest wildflower scent joined a collection featuring warm vanilla, tangy black cherry, fresh linen, and rich toffee apple, to name a few. She'd adapted her formula to use locally sourced organic beeswax from Nigella Turner at Meadowview Garden Centre, adding a sweet, floral edge to the always-fragrant air. The new candles took centre stage as her latest Star Candle of the Month.

She tucked her fair, bobbed hair behind her ears as she turned to show her work to Damon, her best friend and the shop's only employee. The last time she'd checked, he'd been adding discount stickers to the handful of candy cane candles left over from Christmas. Nose buried in a handheld games console, the sticker gun lay abandoned on the floor. Hugo hovered over his shoulder while Damon's fingers danced over the controls to make a tiny, digital Mario bounce on an angry-looking mushroom. The mushroom struck, and they groaned at the 'GAME OVER' screen.

"What do you reckon, Damon?" Claire called. "Think these new beeswax candles will be all the *buzz*?"

"Looking good. And my brain is *buzzing*, trying to get through this level," Damon said, handing the console back to the disappointed eight-year-old. "Sorry, kid. You're on your own with this one."

Sighing, Hugo accepted the console and returned to help his sister, Amelia, with the window display.

"I don't *bee*-lieve you're bad at a video game," Claire said, adjusting one of the wildflower candles to catch the spotlights. "And what do you think the queen bee would do if she caught her worker bees slacking like you are right now?"

"The queen bee doesn't punish or manage the worker bees. Worker bees self-regulate through the hive's social structure, guided by a collective 'wisdom,' and..." Damon's voice trailed off as Claire's eyes glazed over. He hoisted himself off the floor with a groan before pushing his glasses up. "Rhetorical question, wasn't it?"

Claire nodded, pushing at her own sliding glasses.

"And how dare you! I'm never bad at video games," Damon said, rubbing his hands together. "I was up late playing a tricky *Dawn Ship 2* tournament, that's all."

"You could say you have little honey left in the pot for heroic plumbers who save princesses on the side?" Claire elbowed him in the ribs. "Maybe if you'd filled your honeycomb with…" She paused, the pun escaping her. "You know, I think I've run out already."

"Unlike you, I could *wax* poetic with bee puns all day," Damon said, affixing a '20% OFF' sticker on Claire's forehead with the gun.

"Since when are you a bee expert?" Claire ripped off the sticker and jabbed it onto Damon's chin before adjusting the candle he'd put back after giving it a sample sniff. "Or should I ask, what game did you learn all this from?"

Damon's cheeks flushed a deep crimson shade. "I know plenty about plenty outside of games, thank you. And it was *Beekeeper Simulator 3*."

"That riveting they made it thrice?" Claire resisted rolling her eyes before clicking her fingers together when a fresh pun buzzed into her brain. She diverted her attention to the window. "I wonder how my two new worker bees are getting on?"

"So lame," ten-year-old Amelia muttered, shaking her head disapprovingly. "Old people are weird."

"Claire's not *that* old," Hugo said.

"I'm only thirty-six, kids."

"Which is about thirty-four years past your peak in bee years," Damon interjected.

Claire shot Damon—the same age as her—a sideways glance, and he returned to the bottom shelf to finish slashing the prices.

At the window, Amelia, who'd inherited her father's artistic eye, considered each sticker's size and shape before placing it in the right spot. Hugo slapped stickers onto the glass with little restraint, stealing glances at his console between applications. He hadn't taken his eyes off the thing since Claire had collected them for her boyfriend, Ryan, from school.

"This old woman thinks you're both doing a great job." Claire finished the lukewarm coffee that had pushed her through the afternoon restock following the post-lunch shopping rush. "There's a bag of dried wildflowers if you want to arrange them when you're finished."

"I learned in school that child labour is illegal," Amelia remarked, not taking her eyes off her intricate work. "So, how much are you paying us?"

"You offered to do this before Claire even asked," Hugo said.

"Yeah, but you don't ask, you don't get," Amelia fired back. "I'm negotiable, Claire."

"Don't ask, don't get, eh?" Damon called from across

the shop. "How about you double my salary, boss? My stickers are immaculate."

Claire shot him a playful glare. "After catching you playing video games on the job?"

"Fair point."

"How about a Happy Meal for both of you?" Claire suggested to the kids. "And I could even stretch to an ice cream if the machine is working."

"The machine is never working," Hugo muttered as he failed the level again. "But it sounds good to me."

"Don't be so hasty to accept," Amelia said, weighing the value of a Happy Meal and an ice cream against her artistic labour. "We'll consider it and get back to you with a counteroffer."

Before Claire could sweeten the deal with the offer of a milkshake, the door chime jingled, announcing a new arrival. Em, the tattooed yoga instructor with a buzzcut, had a wicker basket of wildflowers resting in the crook of her arm and a bright smile matching the spring sunshine outside.

"Em!" Amelia and Hugo chorused, dropping their work to rush to her.

"Hello, my little yogis," Em said, setting down her basket to scoop them up in a big hug. "The window display looks fantastic from the outside."

"It's a work in progress," Amelia declared, detaching herself from Em to give her creation a critical eye.

5

"And we'll go on strike if you ignore our demands, Claire."

"I won't," Hugo added, tensing a little as Em slipped a daisy into his red-tinged sandy hair after doing the same to Amelia. "Is Dad finished at the gym yet?"

"A couple more hours to go." Em darted her head to Claire, and the two of them stepped to the side. "I just came from the garden centre where your mother is... acting like your mother."

"Oh no. What's she said to you?"

"Nothing to me," Em said, moving closer. "I popped by to see how your father's doing with his new part-time job. Your mother has ground the place to a halt to have everyone search for her purse."

"She's lost her purse?"

"Not according to her," Em said, scratching her prickly hair. "She's accusing someone who works in the café of stealing it."

Claire sighed, already feeling the headache her mother could induce from a mile away. "How did my dad seem?"

"He looked a little embarrassed."

Standing after finishing the discounting, Damon said, "I've got things covered here if you want to finish early."

"Are you sure?"

"I'll hold down the hive for the last few hours," he said,

raising his coffee cup. "Seems you have a sticky situation to fly off to."

Claire removed her nametag and bagged up a few of the new candles, hoping this was all just a misunderstanding. She waved a quick goodbye to Damon, relieved Amelia and Hugo of their free child labour, and ushered them towards the door, hoping her gut instinct about her mother was wrong.

CHAPTER TWO

eeping up with Em and the children, Claire hurried across the quietening shopping square and past Trinity Community Church, where the choir filled the air with springtime hymns. They continued under The Canopies—a local name for Warton Lane—where the trees reached across the road like old friends, their leaves creating a sun-dappled tunnel.

Amelia and Hugo ran ahead, but the steepness of the path forced Claire to acknowledge a twinge of discomfort in her calves. She wasn't as used to the steep lane as she once was. They reached the top of the hill where the old Victorian chimney of Warton Candle Factory loomed over Northash, and she caught her breath. She spotted a group of employees sitting on the wall overlooking the rolling fields of Ian Baron's farm. It was a vantage point Claire had shared with Damon many times during their years at the factory together. If not for the candle shop rescuing them, they would have been there too, still contemplating a future away from the production line.

"You've come a long way," Em remarked, following Claire's gaze. "It's only been a year since you got the keys to your shop, and now look at you."

Claire glanced at Amelia and Hugo, absorbed in a lively debate on the corner up ahead. She had never expected to open her dream shop when she last sat on that wall, but she had fantasised about it for years. And having a boyfriend like Ryan and being a parental figure to his two children? Once eternally single, that had never crossed her mind either, but here she was.

"A long way indeed," Claire said, inhaling one final breath before setting off with a smile. "Wait up, you two. Don't cross the road without me."

Leaving behind the looming factory, the quartet strolled down the tree-lined road towards the turnoff for Meadowview Garden Centre. Nestled down a quaint lane, the garden centre was as welcoming as ever. Flowers of all kinds thrived in small pots stacked on racks around the entrance, and lush hanging baskets swayed in front of the windows, offering a peek inside. No matter the time of day, the place was always teeming with customers, though the police cars parked at jaunty angles were a fresh addition.

"What's going on?" Amelia's eyes widened at the sight of the cars, her youthful imagination racing. "Has someone died?"

"Can we go inside?" Hugo asked.

"How about we look at the fishponds?" Em said, already scooping up their hands. "They have koi carp almost as big as the two of you."

Grateful that Em was taking care of the kids, Claire stepped through the sliding doors of the garden centre. The switch from bright sunlight to dappled shade was jarring, as was the bustling atmosphere. Shoppers, with their trolleys clattering in chaotic harmony, claimed every inch of aisle space. The heady aroma of fresh flowers and the grounding scent of freshly turned soil filled the afternoon air. She'd aimed to capture this very essence in her new fragrance formula, and she was pleased with how close she'd come.

Claire caught sight of her mother, Janet, outside the greenhouse café at the far end of the centre. Hands on her hips, Janet was engaged in an enthusiastic discussion with Detective Inspector Harry Ramsbottom. Bernard Whitman, Meadowview's owner, stood on the sidelines fanning his open palms—nothing too dramatic, yet. Rather than wading right in, Claire pivoted to drop off the bag of candles she'd brought with her.

Following a trail of meandering bees away from the beaten trolley track, Claire found Nigella Turner's beekeeping hideaway in a secluded nook behind the main building. A lively swarm darted and danced, linking the two central hives with a sea of multicoloured wildflowers that seemed to have sprung from an artist's palette. Immersed in her task, Nigella wore a flowing tie-dye shirt tucked into faded, embroidered jeans. She was muttering to herself—or the bees—as she puffed smoke to lull the colony into tranquillity. She pried the hive's lid with measured movements, revealing the intricate dripping honeycomb frames within.

When she caught the beekeeper huffing a heavy sigh over her shoulder, Claire realised Nigella wasn't alone. A tall figure, clad head-to-toe in a white beekeeping suit, leaned against a nearby shed. Gloved hands swatted at the persistent bees with an air of obvious annoyance. Sensing the strain between Nigella and the suited stranger, Claire ducked behind a large tree, not wanting to walk into an altercation.

"I'm telling you, Tom," Nigella insisted, her volume rising, "it *is* Sarah. I'm sure she's stealing my equipment and dipping into the centre's stock. If purses are now going missing, it must be her. Maybe it's time to tell Bernard?"

"You're going to hand Sarah in without firm proof, Nigella?" Tom, the man hidden in the beekeeping suit, dismissed her with a forced chuckle. "You know she's a young mum. Times are tough for us all, but she'll need this job more than anyone. Besides, how can you be sure she's the thief?"

"Call it a gut feeling."

Tom hesitated, and Claire stole a glance. He'd pushed away from the shed and had a hand on Nigella's shoulder. Looking down at the bag in her hand, Claire considered approaching Nigella to break the tension. Her new wax supplier had yet to sample the finished product and had seemed keen to smell them during their previous meeting. Just then, a bee flew over and landed on Claire's bare arm. She froze, not wanting to startle the fuzzy creature.

"Gut feelings can be deceiving, my old friend," Tom said, his tone firm and final. "I know you have your reasons for not trusting Sarah, but maybe it's time to put what happened behind you so you can focus on growing this business."

After a moment of quiet mumbling, Tom hurried past Claire's hiding place, bumping into her before marching around the corner. The bee flew back towards the hives, and Claire hesitated, wondering if she should have gone straight to the café.

"Oh, hi, Claire," Nigella said, looking up from the hive and forcing a smile as Claire stepped out from behind the tree. "Need more wax already?"

"I wanted to drop these off for you," Claire said, holding up the bag. "The first batch using your wax finished curing this morning. I thought you might like to see how they turned out."

"How thoughtful," Nigella replied as Claire approached.

Claire held out the bag, but Nigella's gaze seemed far away. She took a long sip of dark red-tinted tea before setting the cup aside to accept the bag.

"I'm sure they're lovely."

Nigella placed the bag on an upturned crate without taking the jars out to smell them. Claire felt a twinge of disappointment that she didn't want to sample the scent, but she kept that to herself; she couldn't expect everyone to be as obsessed with candles. Nigella busied herself, opening a couple more hives using a smoker to pacify the bees before prying off the lids.

"This is my second beekeeping lesson of the day," Claire remarked, to which Nigella raised an intrigued eyebrow. "My friend told me about bees while avoiding work this morning. Have you heard of *Beekeeper Simulator 3*?"

Nigella's mouth twitched into a polite smile, though her eyes remained clouded as she shook her head.

"He said the queen bee doesn't punish the workers for slacking off," Claire continued, trying to keep the mood upbeat.

"The queen exudes pheromones that compel the workers to serve her every need," Nigella said, a hard edge in her voice. "If a worker bee were ever to step out of line, the rest of the colony would ensure they'd face the consequences. It's unlikely, but the workers can turn against their queen."

"How so?"

Nigella inspected a frame, a dark glint in her eye. "Here's where she lays her eggs. As she ages, her egg-laying capacity will diminish. And when it drops, the workers will create special cells to rear a new queen."

"So, they'll just replace her with a younger model?"

"Exactly," Nigella said with a dry smile. "The new queen that emerges will often kill the old queen or chase her out of the hive."

"That's harsh."

"That's nature," Nigella said, her voice taking on an ominous tone. "Even a once-beloved queen cannot escape the natural order of the hive and the judgement of her subjects. I've seen it happen many times, and it's my job to interfere as little as possible. I monitor them and harvest their wax and honey at the right times."

Claire nodded along, sensing Nigella's mind elsewhere even as she explained the nuances of keeping bees, humouring Claire's curiosity. Nigella finished inspecting the hives and secured the lids before walking into the shed. She returned with a large jar of thick, golden honey.

"A trade for the candles," she offered. "I only work in small batches, but I'll have more wax ready for you soon enough if you sell out, which I'm sure you will."

"Take your time. And thank you for the honey."

Nigella seemed to want solitude, so after a wave, Claire left her amidst the hives and followed her mother's raised voice with her fresh pot of honey in hand. Outside the café, the scene was less sweet and had soured further from when Claire first entered the garden centre.

"You're not *listening*, Harry!" Janet shouted at the DI. "My purse had baby pictures and three hundred pounds in cash from my cleaning jobs. I won't calm down until it's returned to me. I left my handbag on the café counter, and now my purse is gone!"

"And you're sure you didn't—"

"Ramsbottom, if you're about to suggest I 'misplaced' it again…"

Claire bit her tongue, reluctant to fan the flames.

Janet left her threat hanging in the air, and Detective Inspector Harry Ramsbottom seemed to get the message. He jerked back, his pen thrusting into his toupee, as golden as honey against the greying sides. Ramsbottom shifted from one foot to the other, shooting a sidelong glance at Claire's dad, Alan.

Dapper in his green polo shirt uniform, Alan leaned

against his cane for support. He'd clocked in a handful of part-time weekend shifts at the garden centre since the beginning of spring. Meadowview was his favourite place to spend his retirement hours, only second to his pristine garden at home in the cul-de-sac. His face reflected a blend of concern and embarrassment next to Janet's simmering frustration.

Bernard Whitman, the garden centre owner, moved forward, his outstretched palms doing nothing to quell the escalating tension.

"Let's try to keep calm," Bernard stated. "We will find your purse."

Inside the airy greenhouse café, uniformed officers were weaving around sets of tables lined with chequered tablecloths, each adorned with a small vase of fresh flowers. Mismatched chairs and pastel-painted wooden furniture created a cosy atmosphere—a sharp contrast to the tense top notes hanging in the air.

"Check *her*!" Janet exclaimed, pointing at a meek-looking young woman with a blonde pixie cut behind the café's counter. "I know *she* took it."

"Now, Janet, are you sure it was Sarah?" Alan asked, hobbling to his wife's side to rest a calming hand on her shoulder. "It could turn up any second."

"Sarah and I were the only ones in the café after Nigella and Tom left."

"I was here too, Janet," Bernard pointed out. "I was in the corner on my laptop."

"But you weren't paying attention," Janet fired back. "I put my handbag on the counter. I turned my back to answer a call from a new client, and when I went to grab my pen and paper to jot down their address, my purse had vanished from my bag, and—"

"*Found it!*" Behind the counter, a police officer popped up, holding a small leather purse in the air. "It was on the floor under the bottom shelf."

"You must've knocked it off," Sarah explained in a small voice, folding her arms, eyes on the floor. "Simple mistake."

"Oh, you sticky-fingered little swine!" Janet continued, and she would have charged at the waitress if Alan hadn't crossed his cane in front of her. "I paid contactless with my card for some cleaning products before coming here. My card was in my pocket, not in my purse. I didn't take my purse out of my handbag, so how did it end up behind *your* counter?"

DI Ramsbottom, perhaps seeing a quick route out of the awkward gathering, cleared his throat and announced, "Case closed, I'd say?"

Alan, noticing Claire, gave her a subtle nod and let out a relieved breath, perhaps hoping she might defuse the situation.

"Tell them, Claire!" Janet instructed, noticing her too. "I don't just misplace things. I'm an organised person."

Claire felt torn. The overheard conversation by the hives accusing Sarah of being a thief now seemed very relevant, but admitting to eavesdropping could be awkward. And they had found the purse. Claire held her father's gaze for a second, an unspoken conversation passing between them. They both knew—along with anyone working customer service roles in Northash— that Janet's outrage had higher levels that they had yet to unlock.

"It's not like Mum to lose something as important as her purse," Claire began, not wanting to add a sting to the settling chaos. "But we all have moments of distraction, don't we?"

"Oh, you're as bad as your father! You're always looking for a rational explanation. I *know* she stole it. She must have dumped it when she realised I wasn't one to be messed with."

"In my years as a detective," Alan suggested, "jumping to conclusions did no one any favours."

Bernard clapped his hands together, pulling everyone's attention back to him.

"Well, I think we've all learned a valuable lesson about ensuring our personal items are secure," he announced. "Sarah, get back to work. I don't pay you to stand idly around. And Janet, your next order is on the house... for the confusion."

"I'm *not* confused," Janet grumbled, though her rage ebbed as she counted through the money. "Hmm. All present."

Alan tugged DI Ramsbottom aside as they watched the officers leave the café. Meanwhile, Janet stalked Sarah with a withering glare. Sarah, her back turned, continued wiping down the tables as if she hadn't been accused of stealing a customer's purse.

Nigella walked into the greenhouse, cradling her teacup. Her face had turned a pale shade that could outdo even the softest petals. Beads of sweat glistened on her forehead as though she'd been sprinting laps around the garden centre since Claire had left the hives.

"Nigella? Are you okay?"

"I'm fine, Claire," Nigella stammered, sounding anything but. "Had a call from my soon-to-be ex-wife, that's all. She's stressing me out, making all sorts of accusations..."

The teacup slipped from her shaking hands and shattered against the tiles. Claire bent to collect the fragments, but Bernard was quicker. He beckoned Sarah over with a flick of his hand.

"You should head home. You look beat," Bernard advised, holding the broken cup pieces in his palm.

"No, I've still got work at the hives," Nigella said,

popping open a glass-fronted fridge to snatch a water bottle. "I'll be okay. Really."

Sarah swooped in with a broom and dustpan, sweeping up the remnants of the teacup. She then mopped the spilt tea with a white cloth. As Sarah scrubbed away, Claire noticed odd bits entangled in the cloth's fibres. She found herself wondering what sort of tea could leave such peculiar residue. But before she could look closer, Sarah bundled up the cloth and departed, just as Claire's father wandered back.

"I've got a few more hours here yet, and I don't want to leave them in the lurch. Why don't you take your mother home?"

"I'm not losing the plot, Alan," Janet said with a defeated sigh. "You're all making me out to be as batty as Mrs Beaton. But yes, I'll leave you to it." She kissed him on the cheek and added, "Cottage pie for dinner, so don't be too late home."

Claire snuck a final glance over her shoulder at the café as she guided her mother to the exit. Nigella had slumped into a chair in the café and seemed to be tracking Sarah's every movement. Claire was sure her mother, always so meticulous, wouldn't misplace something so important. Still, Claire chose not to confuse the easing conflict as Amelia, Hugo, and Em joined them by the exit.

21

"How were the fish?" Claire asked as they piled into Janet's Angel's cleaning van.

"Massive," Hugo said.

"One was dead," Amelia added.

"Merely sleeping," Em said, positioning Hugo on her knee while Amelia crammed between Em and Claire. "Sorted?"

Claire nodded.

"No," Amelia replied, jabbing a finger into Claire's soft thigh. "We never reached a deal. Happy Meal, and an ice cream, *and* a milkshake."

Claire tapped a finger against her chin, pretending to consider the deal. "You drive a hard bargain, kid, but you worked hard for it." They shook on it. "Can we swing through the drive-thru on the way, Mum?"

Janet nodded as she brought the engine to life with a twist of the key, sparing them the 'it's not proper food' rant that had been a staple of Claire's childhood.

As they backed out of the parking space, Claire caught sight of something unsettling in the wing mirror. Sarah and Nigella had moved by the entrance next to the racks of outdoor flower pots. Nigella had a firm grip on Sarah's wrist, and hostility sparked between them for a second before Sarah yanked free. She tossed her green apron, stormed across the gravel, and marched past the van. Nigella picked up the discarded apron, clenching it as she watched Sarah go.

A knot tightened in Claire's stomach.

Juggling new babysitting responsibilities and launching a fresh candle range was already enough. Yet, as the van pulled away from Meadowview's lush landscape and towards the looming golden arches of McDonald's, Claire couldn't shake the feeling that something more sinister was afoot, and it went beyond a simple case of a misplaced purse.

CHAPTER THREE

*C*laire stacked the last of the grease-spotted Happy Meal boxes into the bin, the lingering scent of salty chips clashing with the usual cleanliness of her mother's kitchen. Janet, as usual, went overboard with lemon-scented surface spray, rubbing her sponge vigorously over the dining table as if erasing a crime scene.

"Maybe I was just hungry earlier," Janet said, scrubbing at invisible spots. "I had a very busy day."

"I think we call that *hangry*," Claire interjected, adding a light note to the atmosphere.

"Three enormous offices and four houses over in Chorley," Janet continued, pausing to hang her head a little. "Oh, I am a little embarrassed, Claire."

Her mother rarely showed this level of self-reflection,

but the situation at the garden centre had unsettled her. She'd been talking about it since the crawling McDonald's queue, and then during the drive to drop Em off at her houseboat.

"Nobody likes the idea of being stolen from," Claire said, grabbing a tea towel to dry the streaks. "I'm sure it's already forgotten."

"But perhaps I shouldn't have accused that girl of stealing my purse without firm proof," Janet said, heaving a sigh and tossing her sponge into the sink. "I've probably ruined your father's new job."

"Come on, you know Dad," Claire reassured, placing a comforting hand on her mother's arm. "He's a people person. He'll smooth things over in no time."

Claire watched Amelia and Hugo through the window as they burned off their Happy Meals in the back garden. Amelia was in hot pursuit of Hugo, a frog triumphantly stretched out in her hand. A wave of contentment washed over Claire at the sight of Ryan's children playing so freely in the garden of her childhood home. It was as if time had looped back on itself, bringing her and Ryan, frog included, to the present.

"I've loved seeing your father getting out and about," Janet said, her voice almost drowned out by the gush of water filling the kettle. "It was a real mental hurdle for him to use that walking stick outside the house. But something changed after he watched those old tapes—"

"What tapes?" Claire interjected.

"Some old VHS home videos from your childhood. You and Ryan are in them. And Ryan's mum." A sad smile passed her lips as she glanced up at the ceiling. "Found them in a box while I was organising Christmas decorations a few weeks ago. Oh, you should've seen your dad's face. Seeing himself as a young officer running around the cul-de-sac without needing the cane did something to him. I feared it might send him into another reclusive spiral. But it motivated him to get back out there. I hope my slip-up hasn't undone all that progress."

Claire couldn't help but feel a sense of pride at the thought of her father in that green polo shirt, once again in a work environment. Since his limp had ended his career in the police force, he'd largely confined himself to garden pottering.

"Dad won't hold a grudge," Claire assured, reaching for two mugs from the cabinet. "And yes, Mum, you have a mouth—big, enormous, vast enough to—"

"Spit it out."

"Don't be too quick to dismiss your gut feeling about Sarah," Claire suggested.

Janet's eyes widened. "Why? What do you know?"

Claire gripped the sink and looked out to the garden. The children had retreated to the far end near the shed, and the frog appeared to blink at her from the patio table.

"I overheard Nigella and Tom arguing about Sarah when I first got to the garden centre. Nigella brought up a missing purse and seemed to insinuate that if there's a thief among them, it's Sarah."

"And you're telling me this now?" Janet tossed teabags into the cups with a huff, ignoring Claire's preference for coffee. "Sometimes, I don't know where I went wrong with you. Why didn't you mention that to DI Ramsbottom?"

Claire envisioned the detective's toupee tilting sideways as her mother's annoyance resurfaced. She was relieved she'd held her tongue back at Meadowview. Given that the purse had been found, blurting out her suspicions would have put her and Nigella in an awkward position.

"You were on edge, Mum, and Sarah looked like she wanted the ground to gobble her up. I didn't want to make things worse."

The kettle reached a boiling crescendo, and Janet lifted it off the base. "So, spill the beans about Sarah. Is she Northash's answer to Bonnie and Clyde?"

"Well, not exactly. Nigella suspected her of taking beekeeping supplies. Some tall guy named Tom persuaded her not to act without concrete evidence. Mind you, I was eavesdropping, so maybe I shouldn't even be talking about this."

A touch of steam curled from the mugs as Janet set

them on the table, sitting across from Claire. For a moment, she stared into the depths of her tea with a look so stern Claire half-expected a grounding and a retreat to her childhood bedroom—now a guest room.

"That'd be Tom Middleton," Janet revealed, her expression easing as she blew on her tea. "He's Nigella's business partner in the beekeeping venture. They were here for dinner last weekend. Stayed up late in the shed with your dad, drinking whisky and hanging onto his detective tales."

Claire let out a chuckle, picturing the scene vividly. "If Dad's been making new friends, there's probably not much to worry about. Nigella said she's going through a divorce, so she must be familiar with difficult wives."

Janet's lips tightened for a moment, then melted into a warm smile. "You've got a point. I hope you're right, love. It'd be a shame if I've unwittingly messed things up right when your dad's getting back into—"

The iconic opening riffs of AC/DC's 'Back in Black' blasted from the garden, shattering the tranquillity of the usually quiet cul-de-sac.

"What the...?" Janet, sloshing tea from her mug, dashed to the back door and squinted out. "Is that noise coming from your dad's shed?"

Claire followed, peering down the garden path to the small wooden shed nestled against the fence, shaded by an old oak tree. Its door hung open, revealing the source of the rebellious tune.

"Chemicals and sharp objects, for heaven's sake!" Janet thrust her half-full mug into Claire's hands and bolted outside. "Kids, what in the world are you—"

The music's volume surged, nearly drowning out Janet's ranting as she quick-stepped over the flat stones set into the immaculate lawn. Claire trailed behind more leisurely, drinking in the tangerine hues of the setting sun as it cast long shadows from the distant factory high on the hill. In his retirement, her dad had transformed his garden into a showpiece that rivalled Meadowview, the perfect playground for his green fingers.

Stepping into the cluttered shed, where cobwebs and thick layers of dust usually kept Janet at bay, Claire found Hugo sitting on an upturned terracotta pot—the same pot that had been Claire's perch for years. Absorbed in his handheld game, Hugo barely looked up while Amelia spun around in Alan's swivel chair at the potting desk.

"I specifically told you children not to come in here," Janet exclaimed, cutting off the radio mid-lyric. "Just look at this mess."

"Nope, you didn't," Amelia countered, unfazed. "This place was messy to begin with."

"I'm quite sure I did."

"You really didn't, Mrs. Harris," Hugo said, adopting a more courteous tone than his sister. "It's cool in here."

Claire felt a pang of nostalgia. Aside from her cosy candle shop, this cluttered shed was her other haven in Northash. Yet, without her father, the space felt incomplete, almost foreign.

Amelia brought the spinning chair to a sharp standstill and pointed towards the back wall. "What's that? Looks like a weird mood board."

While Janet busied herself with putting away garden tools, Claire followed Amelia's finger to a sprawling corkboard wedged between a chainsaw and hedge trimmer. The board teemed with pinned photos, scribbled notes, and assorted paper scraps like receipts and online auction listings. Even at a passing glance, Claire recognised her father's meticulous approach to investigating.

Setting the mugs on a workbench, Claire let her thoughts wander. Forced into early retirement, her dad had found it difficult to abandon his role as a detective inspector. Had it not been for that brain surgery—the one that botched the nerves in his foot—he'd probably still be carrying the DI badge that was now Harry Ramsbottom's burden. Though his foot may have failed him, his mental sharpness remained mostly undiminished.

Claire took a few steps closer to the corkboard. Grainy security footage showed Sarah, the accused waitress, lingering near the beehives—after hours, if the timestamps were anything to go by. Other snapshots caught her outside the café, in the aisles of the tool section, and most damningly, hauling bags out the front doors.

"Unbelievable," Janet declared, leaning over Claire's shoulder.

"More like un-*bee*-lievable," Amelia quipped, giving the radio's dial a twist before resuming her chair spinning. "*Buzzzzz.*"

Claire adjusted her glasses and scrutinised the online auction listings displayed on the corkboard. The evidence was telling, from beekeeping suits to garden tools and bags of coffee beans. "Looks like Dad's been investigating Sarah. You might've been onto something, Mum."

"Oh, there's no 'might' about it," Janet said, her hands planting on her hips. "He might have played devil's advocate, refusing to take my side, but this is irrefutable proof he's suspected her all along."

"Still, there could be more to the story," Claire suggested, despite the growing evidence suggesting otherwise. "Dad always has his reasons. Besides, he usually takes your side."

"And yet you both left me hanging out to dry like yesterday's washing," Janet shot back.

"Speaking of dirty laundry," Claire observed, gesturing at a particular photograph on the board.

"Doesn't it seem like Sarah and Nigella are getting a bit too close in this picture?"

Janet squinted at the photo, where Sarah leaned against the shed and Nigella hovered over her, their faces mere inches apart. "Nigella's practically old enough to be her mother! What on Earth is your dad investigating?"

Hearing the doorbell, Claire glanced at her watch. She left her mother engrossed in the corkboard's mysteries and headed back into the house. Opening the front door, she found Ryan in his gym work attire, eyeing the 'FOR SALE' sign planted in the garden of the house he grew up in next door.

"Still can't believe that place hasn't sold yet," Ryan said.

"Mum's worried about getting the neighbours from hell when it does sell," Claire said. "Told her she might actually be that nightmare neighbour."

Ryan winked, his calm smile sending a warm ripple through Claire. "Ah, your mum was always fine when I lived there. It was her daughter who was the real troublemaker."

"You loved it."

With a quick kiss, Ryan lifted her off the ground. It was something he hadn't managed when they were kids —both of them too 'fluffy' as her gentle dad would say, considerably kinder than her mother's blunt assessments —and living side-by-side. Working as a personal trainer in a gym, Ryan had long since shed the extra pounds Claire had learned to live with. No matter the surrounding chaos, Ryan always had a knack for planting her in the present moment. She never felt more like her true self than when she was with him.

"So, what's the word on the street about you forcing my kids into child labour?" Ryan asked, setting her back on solid ground. "Damon let the cat out of the bag."

"I paid them with Happy Meals, fair and square," Claire defended herself. "Though I still owe them ice cream and milkshakes. The machine was on the fritz."

"How about we all go to the cinema tonight? After teaching that last spin class, I could use a pick-me-up. Half the class was sniffling with hay fever, and the rest were getting irate from all the sneezing, and I have to do it all again tomorrow."

"Yet another reason for me to steer clear of gyms," she joked. "The cinema sounds brilliant. I should get going before Dad comes home. He's in for a grilling from Mum over something she's found in his..." She squinted as headlights cut through the dusky evening. "Ah, speak of the devil. There he is."

Her father drove into the cul-de-sac and parked haphazardly behind the cleaning van. He climbed out of the car, putting more weight on his cane than usual. Spotting them on the doorstep, he tried for a smile that didn't quite reach his eyes, and Claire regretted reassuring her mum that the garden centre fiasco would blow over.

"You're back early, Dad. All good?" As Claire received a kiss on the cheek, she whispered near his ear, "Heads up, Mum's been snooping in the shed."

Alan nodded, saying nothing. That bad of a day? Taking his arm, Claire noticed his drooping posture and the weary look in his eyes as they headed inside. This was about more than the awkward incident with the purse at the café. Something was clearly amiss.

He sagged into a dining room chair with an audible sigh just as Hugo and Amelia burst into the room, their faces brightening at the sight of Ryan.

"Hey there, kids," Ryan greeted, ruffling their hair. "Up for the cinema? I hear an ice cream and milkshake debt needs to be settled."

"*Two* milkshakes," Amelia corrected, flashing the matching number of fingers. "Late fees apply."

"You never mentioned late fees before," Hugo chimed in.

"It was in the fine print."

Janet hurried in from the garden, heading for the kitchen. She shot a tight-lipped glance in Alan's direction, then used her hip to nudge open the warming drawer beneath the oven. From it, she retrieved a grease-stained, crumpled brown bag.

"Don't get your hopes up for cottage pie," she

announced, setting the bag before Alan. She looked at her husband for the first time, her expression changing as she sat beside him. "What's going on? You look awful."

"Could you pour me some whisky, love?" Alan asked Claire, his voice scratchy and tired. "Ryan, would you mind taking the children to the garden? This isn't a conversation for young ears."

Ryan ushered the kids out, and Claire swiftly retrieved the eighteen-year-old Ledaig single malt she'd gifted her father last Christmas. She poured a measure into a crystal tumbler and pushed it towards him. Her pulse quickened as she spotted his trembling hands. He drained the tumbler in one gulp, then locked eyes with them.

"I've got some terrible news," he began, his forehead crinkling as he stared into the emptied glass. Claire refilled it, and he downed that one just as fast. "After wrapping up at the garden centre, I went over to Nigella's beehives for a quick word."

"Did she admit Sarah's a thief?" Janet interjected.

"I wish it were that straightforward."

Pausing, Alan's hand shook as he reached for the bottle. He filled his glass again, but it never reached his lips this time.

"Dad?"

"I found her lying in the soil," he uttered.

Claire's stomach churned through the quarter

pounder and fries. What could have happened to Nigella, the woman who supplied her with beeswax? She hadn't seemed in the best shape when they'd parted at the garden centre.

"Alan?" Janet's voice softened. "Is she in the hospital?"

"She will be," Alan answered, his voice raspy. His finger traced the rim of his tumbler as a darkness clouded his empty stare. "In the morgue. Nigella Turner is dead."

CHAPTER FOUR

The next morning, Claire unlocked her shop to the sound of the clock tower chiming eight times, announcing the start of another shopping day in Northash. Cradling her extra-strong coffee, she flicked on the spotlights, bathing the shop in warm light. Normally, the comforting scent of coffee blended deliciously with the rich scents of the candles, but today, the aroma seemed off; the beeswax added an intrusive note that soured the mood, a hangover from the unsettling events of the previous night.

Damon's singing wafted in from the back room, his off-key melodies grating more than usual. It felt too joyful, too carefree, given the circumstances.

Claire had hardly known Nigella—they were business acquaintances at best and relatively recent ones. But

Nigella had been passionate about beekeeping like Claire was about candle making, which had been a solid enough foundation for her to like Nigella.

Before Claire could drift too far into her thoughts, a crash echoed from the stockroom. While Damon had some skill in candle making, his true talent resided in managing accounts and inventory. She appreciated his enthusiasm for starting on the summer samples to give her the morning off—using her tried-and-true formulas, of course—but cleaning up after his occasional clumsiness wasn't high on her to-do list this morning.

"Everything alright back there?" Claire called out, absentmindedly adjusting jars on the shelves.

"Everything's peachy. Might have dropped a box of wicks and some wax pellets, but it's all under control."

"Are you sure?"

"We trained in the same factory, didn't we?"

Resisting the urge to remind him they'd mostly slapped on stickers back in the day, Claire immersed herself in arranging the display. She meticulously wiped and buffed the jars until they were free of fingerprints. She scrubbed away, finding a comforting rhythm with the task until each polished surface gleamed more than the last. The whole process made her feel like her fusspot mother. By the time she'd added the final touch—a freshly shined flame emblem etched onto the shop's door window—Damon had yet to emerge.

The first customer of the day, Eugene Cropper, sauntered in, his flamboyant floral shirt and dazzling smile lighting up the room. The former politician turned community theatre star was never one to fade into the background.

"Claire, darling!" Eugene greeted, air-kissing both of her cheeks while keeping her at a comfortable arm's distance. "I've just heard this horrid business about you finding that poor beekeeper. You must be terribly shaken. How are you holding up?"

"Word does get around, doesn't it?" Claire replied. "Thanks for asking, but my dad found her, actually."

"In that case, do pass along my heartfelt condolences," Eugene said, releasing her. His gaze then wandered to the candles gracing the central display. "Hold on, are these *the* candles?"

"*The* candles?"

"The ones made from her last batch of wax?"

Claire followed Eugene's keen observation to the Star Candle of the Month display. It was the only area she hadn't yet found the heart to reorganise before the doors opened to customers. She'd hoped for a day of pleasant distractions—anything to keep her mind off Nigella—but she should've known her small-town community better.

"You've got a point there," Claire admitted. "They very well might be from her final batch."

"Sounds like you've got a real collector's item on your

hands." He snatched up a basket and added the six jars from the peak of the spiralling display. "Mark my words, they'll sell like hotcakes. People can't resist their morbid fascination." He glanced into the basket and winked. "I'm not one of them, mind you. Marley can't get enough of floral scents."

For a moment, Claire considered pointing out that Marley, known for his vegan menu at the café around the corner, might not be thrilled about candles made from animal by-products. But she bit her tongue, choosing instead to offer a diplomatic smile. No sense in risking the day's first sale.

"You could probably mark these up a bit," Eugene suggested, heaping in fistfuls of wax melts until they nearly buried the jars. "After all, Nigella will be the talk of the town. She was found face down in the soil, was she not?"

"That's what my dad told me," Claire confirmed.

"Do they know how she passed? Natural causes are in the rumour mill, but she was only about fifty, right?"

"Roughly so, yes."

"People don't just drop dead at fifty, do they?" Eugene's words carried an undertone of suspicion.

Claire's mind flashed back to Nigella—her distracted demeanour, shaky hands, and the teacup crashing onto the tiles. As much as she wanted to share these vivid memories, she caught herself. She hadn't spoken to the police yet and didn't want to jump the gun. But she had to give Eugene something to return from his gossip-recovering mission with. Without information, the village would make something up, and they'd already connected Claire to Nigella.

"Here's something to chew on," Claire began cautiously. "Nigella had been talking about thefts at the garden centre. Makes you wonder if her death and the thefts are somehow connected, doesn't it?"

"A *thief*? Do you know who?" Eugene's eyes narrowed.

"Can't say for sure," Claire deflected, fibbing just a little. It was time to steer the conversation in a lighter direction. "What do you make of the new candle scent?"

Eugene picked up one of the candles, closed his eyes, and took a deep, appreciative sniff. "Divine, absolutely divine. This will be perfect for my bath tonight. Marley will moan about headaches, as usual." He paused, perhaps hearing the contradiction behind his lack of 'morbid fascination' shopping as he dumped the full basket on the counter. "Anyway, I should be off. Tell Damon I said hello. That lad stole the show last night at the pub with his karaoke—upstaged me, even!"

Claire's eyes widened at this nugget of news. Damon, her introverted friend, belting out songs at the pub without her? That was almost impossible to believe.

"Take care, and best of luck with the shop today," Eugene said, leaning in for another set of air kisses before heading for the door, his basket now a bag full of scented treasures. "And Claire, the new window display is stellar. Stick the front page in your window when the *Northash Observer* hits the stands. You can't buy marketing like that!"

"I'll think about it," Claire said, her voice tinged with uncertainty.

Eugene left, but his words hung in the air like an uneasy fragrance. Normally, his effervescence lifted her spirits, but today it had a different effect. It had made her uncomfortably aware that she was becoming the talk of the town, linked to Nigella's untimely end. If the whispers brought in more customers, then it could be a price worth paying. But her real hope was that the police would soon put the case to bed, cross their t's and dot their i's, and let life in Northash get back to normal.

Turning her attention to the silent storeroom, Claire quietly made her way to the door and took a careful peek. Damon was dozing in the battered leather armchair they'd salvaged from a skip in the back alley last month. He was snoring lightly, mouth agape. A tub of fragrance oils sat untouched on the counter, and a box of wicks was strewn across the floor. Claire nudged the bin with her foot and couldn't help but enjoy the sight of Damon jolting awake.

"Up late playing *Dawn Ship 2?*" she inquired, one eyebrow raised.

Damon quickly wiped the drool from the corner of his mouth. "Erm, yeah. Just catching forty winks. Nodded off, didn't I?"

"And? Did you win?" she prodded.

"Hmm?"

"The game?" Claire asked, her lips curling into a restrained smile as she leaned casually against the storeroom door frame. "Did you choose Captain Murphy again?"

"Uh-huh," Damon confirmed.

Claire walked over to their cherished bean-to-cup coffee machine and began filling it with fresh beans. "So, if Captain Murphy were to take the mic at karaoke night, what would be her song of choice?"

"Busted," Damon admitted, staggering to his feet with a slight wobble. "I popped over to the pub for a couple of pints of homebrew. I had no idea about Nigella. My eyes were going square from staring at my computer screen, and Sally intervened. Her mum was watching the children, so she basically coerced me into going."

"And which song received this honour?" Claire pressed, delighting in the unfolding story.

"'I Got You Babe,'" Damon confessed, cringing as if reliving an embarrassing memory. "For the record, Sally insisted on singing Sonny's part."

Claire stifled a laugh as the coffee machine whirred, grinding fresh beans for their morning espresso. She couldn't help but imagine a tipsy Damon serenading his girlfriend, Sally, one of her oldest friends. Interestingly, both Claire and Damon had bid farewell to their single statuses around the same time.

"It's the last hangover at work," Damon vowed.

"Don't make promises you can't keep, Cher," Claire said, handing him a mug containing a double shot of espresso. "After the countless hangover shifts we pulled at the factory, it's not like I can be too cross with you. At least one of us had a fun evening."

Damon's face turned sombre. "Ryan mentioned he wanted to take you to the cinema. That didn't pan out, did it?"

Claire sighed, leaning on the counter beside Damon as he stooped to pick up the scattered wicks. "I ended up sleeping over at my parents' place. Dad was still reeling from finding Nigella like that. And Mum seemed at a loss for how to help him. Brought back memories of his detective days, when he'd clam up instead of talking about what he'd seen."

"Understandable," Damon said. "Any new developments from the police?"

"No updates yet. They've been—" Claire paused, her mobile ringing from her back pocket. She pulled it out and glanced at the screen. Her father's name flashed before her eyes. "Hold on. This might be something." She quickly answered the call, a note of urgency in her voice. "Dad? Everything all right?"

Claire stepped back into the shop. Her heartrate kicked up a notch, filling her with anticipation of whatever her father might reveal about the strange situation enveloping Northash.

"Morning, love," her father greeted, his voice tinged with static. "You must have left the cul-de-sac early this morning. How's business?"

"Quite well, actually. Sold six candles so far," Claire replied, "all to Eugene Cropper. Seems I've got a hot commodity on my hands—Nigella's final wax batch."

A stretch of silence followed, leaving Claire questioning whether she should have left out that last detail.

Her father finally spoke. "That's an interesting way to look at it." He cleared his throat. "The police are wrapping up their investigation around the—uh, the beehive area. You were spotted chatting with Nigella there and at the café. They suspect you might've been one of the last to talk to Nigella before she—"

Keeled over into the soil?

"Oh," Claire replied. "Do they want to speak with me?"

"It might offer some context. I'm heading to the garden centre after I've finished my poached eggs. You could join me?"

Claire hesitated, anxiety fluttering in her chest at the

prospect of returning to the very place where Nigella had drawn her last breath. Yet, curiosity tugged at her as well. A part of her yearned to know precisely what the police had unearthed, if anything at all. However, the haunting memory of Nigella's pallid face and trembling hands, clutching that cup of herbal tea, anchored her to her current spot.

"Perhaps I'll pay a visit to the station after my shift," Claire suggested.

"No need to feel pressured, my dear. But I'll be there, regardless of your decision." After a pause, he said, "And frankly, I could use the company. Your mother has been at Starfall House giving the place a thorough top-to-bottom clean all morning."

Claire pictured her father navigating the garden centre alone, leaning on his cane. He seemed to have aged a decade in the few hours following Nigella's death the previous night. He would have known she wouldn't say no to such a plea, but she knew he wouldn't have asked if he didn't genuinely need her. He was taking it hard, blaming himself for not realising something was going on before it was too late.

"I'll come," Claire said, her eyes tightening as she tried to inject some lightness into her voice. "I'd only be answering questions about it here all day."

After ending the call, she briefed Damon, who already halfway through his coffee.

"No problem. I can hold down the fort," he said, less enthusiastically than he had for her previous garden centre trip. "Just don't go getting yourself tangled up in anything dangerous. This shop will need someone to redo these summer samples after I've finished butchering them."

"I'm sure they'll be perfect," Claire reassured him.

"You think so?"

"Don't make a mess," she said with a peck on his cheek, snatching her denim jacket from the hook. "I shouldn't be too long."

"Take your time," he called after her. "And you didn't answer my question."

"They'll be so fantastic, we'll have to rename the shop 'Damon's Candles'."

"Don't push it."

Claire strolled up the lane towards the cul-de-sac, making it as far as the bridge over the canal before encountering her father's car. She hopped in, and they cruised under The Canopies. The short journey to Meadowview Garden Centre allowed Claire's nerves to resurface. As they turned onto the tree-lined lane leading to Meadowview, she glimpsed police tape sectioning off areas. Her hopes of a quick resolution to the case dwindled upon seeing the numerous uniformed figures swarming the area.

Alan parked in his usual spot near the back. Before

they stepped out of the car, he squeezed Claire's hand and said, "Thank you for coming, little one. I know this can't be easy."

"We're here for the same reason."

"The truth," he agreed.

As they moved through the garden centre, police officers in blue gloves litter-picked around potted shrubs and flower beds. Claire spotted Detective Inspector Ramsbottom conferring with a uniformed officer near the row of beehives, arms waving and shoulders hunched. Edging closer, Claire made out snippets of their conversation. She looked around for her father, who had vanished in the crowd of officials, no doubt drawn in by someone he recognised.

"...Foul play's evident here," DI Ramsbottom grumbled. "Interrogate the staff and don't stop until you've done it twice. Someone's got to know if Turner was contemplating this."

The officer jotted down the notes before making a quick exit. Seizing the moment, Claire cleared her throat and stepped forward.

"Excuse the interruption, Detective Inspector, but I couldn't help but overhear."

Ramsbottom pivoted, his eyebrows pulling together and lips taut as if donning a mask of authority. Claire caught the brief flicker of uncertainty in his eyes before he could fully commit to the 'everything's under control' performance.

"Ah, Claire," he said with a throat clearing. "Alan did say you might drop by. Terrible, terrible business, all of this. Did you happen to notice if that burger van up the road was open?"

"I think I took a different route."

"A shame," he sighed, clearly let down. "Now then, you were among the last to see Nigella. Did she perhaps... hint at wanting to end her life?"

"Are you leaning towards suicide?"

"We're trying to rule it out." Ramsbottom cast a quick glance at the forensic team combing through the soil near the shed. "Awaiting the full toxicology report, but my bet is on poisoning. What was your read on her?"

Claire felt a chill, the last flicker of hope that this was a mere accident snuffed out. "Nigella did seem more drained than usual when we spoke yesterday," she said, maintaining a neutral expression. "She was shaky, pale, and mentioned feeling stressed over a call from her wife about their divorce."

"Divorce, eh?" The inspector scribbled this new detail. "Worth a closer look. Anything else?"

"What about the waitress yesterday?"

Ramsbottom sighed. "Janet been filling your ears?"

"Always, but I heard something, too."

Claire recounted the exchange between Nigella and Tom that took place right where they now stood. Ramsbottom filled two pages in his notebook, vigorously underlining 'SPEAK WITH SARAH!!!' before snapping it shut.

"I knew I could count on you," Ramsbottom said, his eyes drifting away from Claire to track an officer who sauntered by with a burger oozing with fried onions and ketchup. "Did anything else catch your eye?"

"I spotted Nigella and Sarah talking as I was leaving. They seemed... close."

"Close? How so?"

Claire weighed whether to mention her father's investigation board stashed away in the shed, featuring the photograph of Sarah and Nigella. She decided against it; if her dad wanted Ramsbottom in the loop, he'd say so himself.

"Nigella had hold of Sarah's wrist," Claire chose to say instead. "Looked like she wanted to have a serious talk. But Sarah yanked her hand back and darted off. What about Tom? Know where he is?"

"Still looking for the business partner," Ramsbottom admitted, shoving his notebook into his pocket, already edging away from Claire, clearly seduced by the aroma of fried onions. "The home we traced to him is empty. Seems he moved out a while ago, but I'm sure he'll surface, eventually. Thanks for stopping by, but we've got it from here. No need to involve yourself further."

Claire felt a prickle of irritation at the casual brush-off but held her tongue. Picking fights wouldn't help, especially after she'd practically filled Ramsbottom's notebook for him.

She found her father, who was deep in subdued conversation with Bernard, the garden centre owner. Standing by the locked café entrance, Bernard looked put-together with his broad shoulders and a well-kept salt-and-pepper beard. But his smile? Too wide and way too forced, considering why they were all here.

"Sorry for your loss," Claire offered. "Were you close to Nigella?"

"Somewhat," Bernard responded, breathing a sigh that felt as rehearsed as his smile. "The beekeeping venture is Nigella and Tom's. I rent them the land. Before her, it was a dumping ground. I trust Tom will keep things going."

"Seen him lately?"

"Should I have seen him?" Bernard arched an eyebrow. "I haven't been able to open the garden centre today because of *this*." He gestured dismissively at the officers shuffling between the flowers. "But Tom will probably show up sooner or later. Someone needs to tend to those bees. Saying that, maybe we should just let them go."

"I don't think it's that simple," Claire said, her eyes narrowing at Bernard, who seemed preoccupied with trivialities. "But as you said, he'll turn up. Heard from Sarah?"

"She quit," Bernard replied, flicking his hand as if swatting away an annoying fly. "She emailed her resignation last night. Likely wanted to dodge any police questions after yesterday. I tried to maintain peace for the customers, but let's be clear: I think she nicked Janet's purse. That's why I had your dad dig into her." He slapped Alan's shoulder with a force that made him wobble. "Good riddance, I say. Always asking for advances and extra shifts. I'm not running a charity here." He then fished out a business card from his suit pocket. "Maybe some good can come of all this. Nigella mentioned she was supplying your candle shop with wax. We spoke about stocking your lovely candles here at the garden centre. Did she mention anything to you?"

Claire hesitated, eyeing the business card before finally taking it. "She didn't."

"Well, if you're interested, let's talk," Bernard leaned in, dropping his voice a notch. "Between us, this place is a gold mine, but diversity never hurts. Our foot traffic is solid, and we don't have to stick to just garden supplies, do we? Candles, jams, honey… The list of random tat—" He cleared his throat and continued, "The list of high-quality items my customer base is willing to buy is endless."

Claire felt her discomfort grow. Had this proposal

come a day earlier, it might have seemed less crass. Holding his business card now felt inappropriate. She slipped it into back pocket and felt its presence like a nagging itch.

"I'll have to think about it," she said, her voice noncommittal. "My stock is somewhat limited right now. We have plenty of online orders these days, so we need to keep levels up."

"Of course, take your time. No rush," Bernard said, his smile faltering as he rested a weighty hand on Claire's shoulder. "But do consider it seriously. I can promise very competitive rates. Increased profits are pretty much a guarantee. Let me escort you both out."

Walking them only as far as the back door, Bernard left Claire and Alan to finish the journey on their own. Neither spoke until they were safely in the car and driving away.

"Found that a bit off as well, did you?" Alan pre-empted Claire. "Bernard is definitely not the man I thought he was after all these years."

Claire wove her fingers together, unease bubbling up. "Dad, why were you investigating Sarah? The board in your shed with the pictures and receipts—did that have something to do with you getting the job at the garden centre?"

"Not the initial reason, no. Bernard complained about some missing stock, so I'd been asking around. Nigella, too, had suspicions and suggested Sarah as a possible culprit. Sarah's a young mother with two kids, and while fingers point her way, there's not enough concrete evidence."

As they pulled into the cul-de-sac, Alan killed the engine and turned to Claire.

"Nigella suspected Sarah, which now makes the waitress a prime suspect, if not *the* prime suspect," Alan said, unbuckling his seatbelt. "I can tell you want answers as much as I do, Claire. As far as I'm concerned, I've already started my investigation. You're welcome to join me."

Claire considered if she wanted to dive in to sleuthing with her father. She wanted to know the truth, but she already had a plate full as it was.

"Can I think about it?"

"Of course," he replied. "Truth be told, if someone is willing to resort to poisoning, I'd rather you stayed out of this one."

"You need to be careful too, Dad."

"You know me, little one," he reassured her, patting her hand affectionately. "I haven't lost my touch. Now, how about I make us some lunch? Then, you can check on your shop and see if those limited-edition candles have flown off the shelves."

The peaceful sanctuary of her parents' garden offered a welcome respite. Claire savoured her sandwiches and tea, letting the spring breeze carry away the morning's tension as she and her father engaged in easy conversation.

As she headed back to her shop, her thoughts shifted. The morning had been fraught with unsettling revelations, but the business wouldn't run itself, and she felt guilty enough as it was for leaving Damon to run things with his hangover.

Time to switch gears.

As she approached the shop, Claire took in the new window display. Bee stickers buzzed around an array of dried flowers and grasses. While not a masterpiece, Damon had done his best to complete what Amelia and Hugo had started.

Yet today, the aesthetics of the window display didn't matter.

Peering through the glass, Claire saw Sally plucking wildflower candles from the upturned crates. Sally caught her eye and gestured for her to come inside, and Claire felt as if she'd entered a different world the moment she stepped in. Eugene's ominous prediction had materialised astonishingly fast. The quiet shop she'd left that morning had transformed into a buzzing marketplace, filled with chatter and nearly devoid of the star candles.

"It's an absolute circus!" Sally said to Claire as she added the window candles to the middle shelf. "I only stopped by to drop off some B12 for Damon's hangover, but I had to ditch my afternoon house viewing. I couldn't leave him to this."

"My fault," Claire apologised.

Feeling suffocated amidst the crowd in her shop, Claire ducked behind the counter. She put on her most gracious smile and deflected the instant questions about Nigella. While she did have updates following her visit to the garden centre, she had no intention of being the town crier about the poisoning incident. Damon, clearly still reeling from his night of karaoke, had a sheen of sweat on his forehead as he thrust a jar right through a paper bag in his hurry.

The safety of the backroom beckoned, but Claire shrugged off the temptation.

Better to face this head-on.

"Damon, take a breather," Claire declared, flexing her fingers as she tore open a new paper bag. "I've got it from here."

CHAPTER FIVE

*C*laire sent Damon on his way as soon as the flow of customers eased off, urging him to head home and crash into bed. After a final hectic stretch, where she deflected Nigella-related questions with the agility of Keanu Reeves dodging slow-motion bullets, Claire closed the shop and strolled around the corner to Christ Church Square. She let herself into the snug, terraced cottage that had once been her Uncle Pat's. Walking down the narrow staircase to Ryan's tiny art cellar—formerly Pat's underground casino—she ducked not to hit her head on the doorframe.

She opened the door to the studio with a creak, the aroma of oil paints blending with the earthy dampness. Ryan was engrossed at his easel, his shirt sleeves rolled up over his well-defined arms, adding splotchy touches to a vibrant vase of sunflowers.

"How cheerful," Claire remarked, sidling up beside him.

"Trying out a new brushstroke technique."

"You seem to have it figured out already," she complimented.

Ryan sighed, stretching his neck. "Haven't had much time to paint lately. These extra shifts at the gym are taking their toll. Feels like all I've been doing is working and sleeping, and today was particularly rough." Pausing, he dipped his brush into a blob of yellow paint on the messy palette. "Sorry, your shop looked jam-packed today. The last thing you need is me moaning about being knackered."

Claire chuckled. "I'll listen to you moan any day of the week. That's what I'm here for, right? Besides, you're the one who's exercising for a living. I stood in one spot, watched people clear the shelves, and let people bombard me with questions about Nigella like I was her next of kin. All because I bought some wax from her."

"That'd be the new limited-edition candle, then?" Ryan asked. "Heard some of my regulars talking about snagging some jars before they all sold out."

"More like 'rare edition,' given our dwindling stock," Claire said, resting her head on his shoulder as she admired the artwork. Ryan's artistic talent, inherited from his late mother, never ceased to amaze her. "So, what made today so rough for you?"

"Our manager upped and left this morning. No notice."

"Yikes."

"He got a better offer working in a spa over in Clitheroe. I've been asked to fill in temporarily. So much for tomorrow's day off." With a shrug, he rinsed his brush and set it aside. "Think I'm done for today. This piece isn't shaping up the way I'd hoped."

Before Claire could assure him that it was incredible to her eye, footsteps thundered down the stairs. Amelia's and Hugo's faces popped through in the doorway.

"Hi, Claire," Hugo greeted. "We're bored."

"Really bored," Amelia chimed in, sounding rather put out. "We were promised a cinema trip yesterday."

Surveying Ryan's tired face, Claire sensed he wasn't up for an excursion but too decent a dad to disappoint the kids. An alternative plan sprang to mind, a touch closer to home, and she could already taste the homebrew.

"How does a trip to the pub sound?" Claire proposed. "Might be a free pool table?"

THE WELCOMING EMBRACE OF THE HESKETH ARMS enveloped Claire the moment she stepped in. She settled into a timeworn leather sofa near the fireplace, savouring a pint of the pub's locally revered Hesketh Homebrew. With the first sip, she knew she'd made the perfect choice for unwinding after a gruelling day. Watching Ryan guide Amelia and Hugo in a game of pool, her heart swelled. His patience in adjusting their hands on the cue sticks was touching.

"Cracking shot, Hugo," Ryan praised as a yellow ball plopped into the corner pocket. "You've got a knack for this."

Amelia exhaled sharply, blowing her fringe out of her eyes. "He's only good because he's glued to games all day. I'll trounce him next round."

"Don't be a sore loser," Ryan said, soft but firm. "There's still time to even the score."

With a slight pout, Amelia relinquished her cue to Hugo and returned to the game. Ryan slid next to Claire on the sofa, sipping his own pint of Hesketh's finest. Seeing him so hands-on with his kids always stirred something tender in Claire.

"Ever thought about throwing your hat in for the manager's position?" Claire ventured.

Ryan frowned. "I'm not sure I've got what it takes. The money and fewer hours are tempting, but I've only been at the gym a little over a year. If the owner thought I was the right fit, he'd have offered me the job already."

"In the words of your daughter, you don't ask, you don't get," Claire said, looking over at Amelia as she carefully lined up her shot. "You work hard, and clients love you. The 'hunky redhead's classes' are all the rage among my customers."

Ryan smiled, his cheeks going a shade rosier. "Earning a bit more would help. I'm barely covering rent and bills, let alone saving for the future." He leaned his head back on the sofa with a groan. "Oh, and I can't pick up the kids from school tomorrow. Reckon they're old enough to walk home?"

"We used to walk home when we were Amelia's age," Claire reminded him, although he looked uneasy. "Want me to pick them up again?"

"I can't ask. You've done it twice this week already."

"It's easier for me to leave the shop than for you to skip out on the gym. Plus, they can go up to my flat if they get bored with being put to work," she said, placing her hand on his thigh. "We're a team, right?"

"You're sure?" Smiling as if surprised by her sentiment, Ryan clasped her hand. "Wouldn't want to be teamed up with anyone else. I really love you, Claire."

"You're not too shabby yourself." Claire grinned, giving his hand a squeeze. "Looks like the kids are wrapping up. How about a game, superstar?"

"Are you challenging me?"

"Prepare for defeat," she said, playfully slapping his knee as she stood. "I won't go easy on you."

"You're on," he shot back, tugging her back onto the sofa before springing to his feet. "Last one to the table sets up."

As Ryan set up the pool table, Amelia and Hugo gravitated back to the sofa. Surrounded by the pub's warm vibe, the clicking of pool balls, and the comforting chatter, Claire felt at home. Even with the shadow of Nigella's scandal still hanging over her, everything seemed just right.

CLAIRE WAS SETTING UP A CHALLENGING BANK SHOT WHEN the pub door burst open, ushering in a blast of crisp evening air. She looked up to see Sally stroll in, trailing a downcast Damon behind her.

"Ah, the karaoke legends return," Claire announced, as she deftly sank a red ball into the side pocket. "Not had enough of your Sonny and Cher duet from last night?"

Damon collapsed into the nearest chair, eyeing the bottles behind the bar with a hint of nausea. "Ugh, don't remind me. I reckon I'm still nursing that hangover."

Perched on a stool beside him, Sally grinned. "Well, you should've taken the B12 I offered you this morning."

She gave his shoulder a playful nudge. "I've not been in top form today either. Makes me thankful I share custody with an ex-husband."

Ryan, preparing for his next shot, chalked his cue. "How's the co-parenting situation?"

Sally glanced at the food menu while Damon sank further into his chair. "Paul's keeping his distance from me and being there for the girls, so I'm giving it two thumbs up. Heard anything from Maya since Christmas?"

Ryan shook his head as he aimed for a yellow ball teetering on the edge of the pocket, but his cue ball skidded past, missing by a considerable margin. Claire gently rested a hand on his shoulder. Maya had signed the divorce papers during a fleeting Christmas visit and then vanished again, leaving the kids behind for a second time in their life.

"We're not here to drink," Sally said, tossing the menu onto the table. "I might just have some juicy intel on Nigella for you."

Claire, potting another red ball, looked up. "Who said I was on the case? And what's this intel you're talking about?"

Sally leaned forward, her eyes sparkling. "You'll want to investigate after hearing this. You know the client appointment I cancelled to help you in the shop? Someone else at the estate agency went to value her property."

"And this client is?"

"Fiona Turner?"

Claire raised an eyebrow. "Should that name ring a bell?"

Damon whipped out his mobile, scrolled through his Facebook app for a moment, and then handed it to Claire. The screen showed a wedding photo: Nigella, radiant in a white wedding gown, had her arm wrapped around a smiling auburn-haired woman, also in white.

"Turner," Claire murmured. "Nigella's wife."

"She's keen to undervalue for a quick sale," Sally added.

Claire's mind raced as she grappled with the new intel. Fiona was looking to offload their shared home just one day after Nigella's death? She cleared the table to win the game, but any sense of victory was overshadowed by her racing thoughts.

"Did Fiona seem distraught or mention Nigella at all?" Claire questioned.

Sally paused to think. "I heard she seemed a bit frazzled and distant. But honestly, that's not unusual when people are about to sell their homes. The connection to Nigella didn't click until Damon and I were grabbing some fish and chips."

Damon switched to another post on Fiona's Facebook timeline, dated New Year's Eve. The photo captured Nigella and Fiona in matching sparkly hats, their smiles strained as they celebrated at The Park Inn's annual party. Unlike their wedding picture, a noticeable gap separated the two. Claire's mind flashed to that photo of Nigella and Sarah she'd seen in her father's shed.

Damon broke the silence. "Couldn't find Nigella on social media, but Fiona changed her relationship status from 'married' to 'single' in the second week of January. She's kept all their pictures up, but scrolling back over their ten years of marriage, Fiona has barely included her in any posts in recent years. Just the usual 'keeping up appearances' around the important dates kind of stuff."

Claire felt her pulse spike. "What if their separation has something to do with Nigella's death?"

"Steady on." Ryan, who had been listening on the sidelines, started massaging Claire's shoulders. "Could it just be a coincidence?"

But Claire's detective instincts were already zeroing in. She sensed a potential motive and knew she had to dig deeper into Nigella and Fiona's relationship.

Sally and Damon returned to their quiet evening alone, and after soundly beating Ryan at pool three games in a row, Claire ushered Amelia and Hugo out of the pub with a promise of ordering pizza at her flat. Amelia and Hugo sprinted ahead as they hit the cobbled square, veering around opposite sides of the clock tower on their way to the candle shop.

"Can't stop thinking about the beekeeper mystery?" Ryan asked, interlocking his fingers with Claire's.

"A little," Claire began, reconsidering, "Actually, a lot. I should call my dad. He's got an inside track on this case. He was looking into—"

"Hey, there's something on your doorstep!" Amelia's voice cut through Claire's thoughts. "Looks like jam."

"It's not jam, it's honey," Hugo corrected.

Claire and Ryan looked puzzled at each other before quickening their pace to catch up with the kids. Sitting on the shop's doorstep was a pint-sized jar of golden honey adorned with a bold red ribbon. Hugo picked it up and handed it to Claire, who laughed nervously. Her stomach churned as she read the note attached: 'MIND YOUR BEESWAX, BUSYBODY!'

"Late-night delivery?" Ryan asked, shooting Claire a questioning look. She shook her head in reply. "Anything concerning?"

Amelia interjected, "What's more concerning is what's going on the pizza?"

"Ham and pineapple," Hugo suggested.

"Disgusting," Amelia said, leaping onto the doorstep to jiggle the locked door handle. "Pepperoni only. And remember, you owe us ice cream and milkshakes, Claire."

"I haven't forgotten, I promise," Claire said, her fingers tightening around the jar. Her smile strained, adding, "Sort the pizza. I need to swing by the cul-de-sac for a moment. I'll be back in ten minutes."

Ryan's eyebrows knitted together. "Should we come with you?"

"I'm starving!" Amelia wailed. "Especially for ice cream and milkshakes."

"Just ten minutes," Claire reiterated, planting a quick kiss on Ryan's lips. "Don't scoff all the garlic knots without me."

Once Ryan and the kids were inside the flat above the candle shop, Claire sped toward her parents' cul-de-sac, her mind whirring as the sky bled into evening ink. Once inside, she caught the distinct timbre of her mother's interrogative voice wafting from the sitting room. It sounded like she was in the middle of interviewing a potential new cleaner for Janet's Angels. Unwilling to interrupt, Claire opted for the soft, stealthy exit she'd perfected as a teen and closed the door to sneak down the side of the house to the back garden.

She found her father in his shed, creasing his brow at his investigation board.

"Ah, twice in one day?" Alan greeted her, his face lighting up.

Setting the jar of honey down on a potting bench, Claire said, "I come bearing gifts—or warnings, perhaps. This was left on my doorstep."

Alan's expression shifted to one of concern as he examined the note. "Any idea who left it?"

"No clue," Claire said, folding her arms as she scanned the investigation board speckled with photos of Nigella, Sarah, and others. "But it feels like a threat."

Alan returned the jar to the table and sank into his swivel chair. "I suppose you've helped solve enough mysteries around Northash that even showing up at a crime scene rattles some people. Seems someone wants you off the scent."

"I hadn't even dipped a finger in this particular honey pot," Claire quipped, aiming to lighten the heavy atmosphere. Her father's gaze remained fixed on the jar. "So, about earlier. You asked if I was in?" Alan started to speak, but Claire cut him off. "I'm in," she affirmed, positioning herself before the board.

Alan sighed. "This makes me uneasy, Claire. Perhaps we should let the police handle this."

"And you think Ramsbottom will solve this?" Claire focused on the pictures of Nigella and Sarah. "You're already looking into Sarah. She's suspicious. And Bernard? He's eager to move on like it's all water under the bridge. And where's Tom, for that matter?"

Alan nodded. "All valid points."

"We can solve this, Dad. Together. Before someone else gets hurt."

Her father paused, weighing his choices.

"We proceed cautiously," he finally said, gently squeezing her shoulder. "The last thing I want is for something to happen to my daughter. We need to take this honey to the station for testing. Who knows? The second poisoning might already be in the works."

Leaving her father in his shed, Claire walked to the local police station near Sally's house and left the jar of honey with a disinterested desk officer. He barely glanced up from his mobile as Claire explained the situation. After prying a vague assurance from him that they would test it for poison, she stepped back into the chill of the evening.

She arrived at her shop just as the delivery driver pulled up. Balancing a stack of warm pizza boxes in her arms, she unlocked the door and was greeted by the heavy scents of wildflowers. Despite nearly selling out her new stock and raking in a tidy sum, Claire hoped the local curiosity would wear off to give way to a more routine day tomorrow.

Upstairs, Domino coiled around Claire's ankles, meowing for attention. She placed the pizza boxes on the kitchen counter. From the living room, Sid's eyes peeked over the sofa, where Amelia and Hugo fought over the remote. Ryan stepped out of the spare room, freshly made beds awaiting their increasingly frequent young guests. As he joined her in the kitchen, she plucked a garlic knot from the top box and popped it into his mouth.

"All sorted?" he inquired.

"Not quite," Claire admitted. "But it will be. So, what's on the telly tonight, kids?"

Claire had no idea what the next day would bring, but with her dad's expertise and Ryan's support, she felt up to the task. For tonight, the swirling suspicions could wait; her focus was on the simple joy of a family pizza night.

CHAPTER SIX

*a*fter Ryan left to take the kids to school before his long day at the gym, Damon arrived at the shop with no sign of a karaoke hangover. When Claire ventured downstairs ten minutes before opening—having waited her turn for the shower—Damon greeted her with a hearty sandwich of sausage, bacon, and egg, all smothered in ketchup.

"Managed an early night, just for you," he said, handing her a cup of black coffee. "I'll be fine watching the shop for the morning."

"Aw, you're a gem, Damon."

"You should think so. According to Sean in the group chat this morning, I missed a 'legendary' *Dawn Ship 2* tournament."

They unpacked the penultimate box of wildflower candles as they enjoyed their breakfast and strong coffees. Claire took the honours of unlocking the shop and flipping the sign to 'Open,' then headed out. As planned, her father's car was parked outside the fish and chip shop.

"Morning, little one," Alan greeted her, his face lined with fatigue; dark circles under his eyes bore witness to a restless night. "Called ahead last night. Sarah is expecting us."

"Willingly?"

"She sounded wary," he said as he drove past Claire's Candles, "but it's a positive sign that she agreed to speak with us."

Alan drove down Park Lane, the trees lining the edge of Starfall Park glowing golden in the morning sun. He swung around the roundabout and onto the slip road, and before Claire knew it, they had merged onto the motorway, fields and farms blurring past.

Rather than thinking about the case, Claire wondered how she'd got so close to asking Ryan to move in with her the previous night. Once the children had shuffled off to bed, yawning and bleary-eyed, she and Ryan had stayed up talking on the sofa until close to midnight. They talked about nothing and everything. And, as usual, when they were alone for long enough, they reminisced about their teenage years as friends, back when Ryan had lived next door in the cul-de-sac.

The teenage Claire would never have believed that the boy she'd missed for years, the one who moved to Spain and swept her dreams away with a Spanish beauty, was now her boyfriend. A man who held her hand and told her he loved her at every opportunity.

Claire relished the nights when Ryan and the children stayed at her flat. She found herself inviting them more and more these days. She yearned for the comfort of falling asleep beside Ryan and waking up to cook breakfast together—though he was the much better cook of the two. The suggestion to move in together had been on the tip of her tongue last night, but the moment had slipped away undiscussed.

As residential streets replaced the motorway, she considered asking her father what he thought about taking the next step with Ryan. But then she realised they were slowing to a crawl.

"Here we are," Alan announced, peering up at the tower block.

The building, which must have been thirty storeys high, loomed over them, a monolith of grey concrete and black windows. Graffiti tags marked the lower levels; higher up, satellite dishes hung precariously off the sides of balconies. The grounds around the building were barren:, with not a tree or bench in sight, just patches of dead grass and litter swirling in the wind. It was a stark contrast to the quaint shops and tidy homes of Northash, just a few miles away. Claire felt a chill as she looked up at the soaring structure, imagining how isolated and detached she might feel living in the tower's gloomy confines.

"Lowry Tower," Alan said, marching forward with his cane. "Conducted more than my fair share of interviews here over the years. Almost nostalgic to be back. She's in flat 308. Which, if memory serves, is up top. Let's hope the lift works, eh?"

They took the lift—thankfully, in working order—to the second-to-top floor, where Alan knocked on the peeling blue door of flat 308. It opened, revealing Sarah in a grey hoodie and leggings, her blonde pixie cut tousled as though she had just woken up. Claire had barely interacted with her at the garden centre's café the day of the purse accusation, but there was a flicker of recognition in her eyes.

"Morning, Sarah," Alan said cheerily. "Thanks for agreeing to meet with us."

"Morning," Sarah said quietly, glancing between them with uncertainty. "You said you had some questions for me? If this is about your wife's purse—"

"A matter that's been dealt with," Alan insisted, raising

his free hand. "This is about Nigella Turner. You were her colleague at the garden centre, and the two of you were seen talking here and there."

It struck Claire that she'd never accompanied her father during one of his interviews in his detective days. Considering the information about Sarah displayed on his shed wall, she was impressed by his tact.

Still, Sarah's eyes darkened at the mention of Nigella's name, but she stepped aside to let them into the cramped flat. Claire glanced around as they entered the dim living room. The worn furniture had clearly seen better days, and a small TV flickered in the corner, playing a colourful cartoon that two young children were transfixed by as they sat on the floor.

"Can I get you something to drink?" Sarah asked. "I've just brewed a pot of tea."

Both declined politely as Sarah gestured for them to take a seat at the small dining table. They sat, and Alan began asking Sarah about her previous job at the café.

"I didn't steal anything, if that's what this is about," Sarah said defensively, crossing her arms over her chest. "Not your wife's purse. Not anything. I'm no thief."

"We believe you," Alan said gently, though Claire wasn't sure if he meant it. "The purse was found, after all. But we've also heard there were additional accusations of stolen items being traced back to you—beekeeping equipment, tools, things from the café. Can you shed any light on that?"

Sarah's knee bounced under the table. "It's all lies. The job was bad enough without being accused of things I didn't do."

Claire studied the young woman's face, but Sarah was avoiding their gazes. She asked, "If the rumours aren't true, why did you quit after Nigella died?"

"I quit *before* I heard Nigella had died," Sarah said, brushing a stray hair from her eyes. "And it was time for a change. The management, the customers, the gossip—it had turned into a toxic environment. I wasn't coming home in the best mood after work." She gestured to the little boy and girl still glued to the TV. "I needed to do what was best for my family."

Claire nodded. She wanted to believe Sarah, but surely keeping her job would have been the best thing for her family. Rather than pointing that out, she thought back to what she'd seen in the wing mirror as her mother had driven her away from the garden centre.

"We've heard that you and Nigella had some conflict shortly before her death," Claire said, taking her father's tactful approach. "Nigella had a hold of your arm, and you were seen throwing your apron on the floor after you pulled away from her. Can you tell us about that?"

At the mention of Nigella's name, Sarah's expression

changed. Her eyes grew distant, and her jaw tensed. "We had a disagreement, yes. But I fail to see how that's important now. I didn't poison her."

"We never said she was poisoned," Alan pointed out.

"No, but the police did," she fired back, frowning. "You think you're the first ones round here asking me questions?"

Alan's cheeks flushed, and Claire wondered if her dad had forgotten he wasn't an actual detective anymore. He cleared his throat and offered an apologetic smile. Claire hesitated, debating whether to reveal that she'd overheard the argument between Tom and Nigella that day in the garden centre. She opted for a softer approach.

"There's a photograph of you with Nigella," Claire said, "by her beekeeping shed. You looked quite close in the picture."

Alan produced the picture from his inside pocket. Sarah glanced at the image, and her cheeks flushed pink.

"It was nothing. She went through a messy split with her wife and got clingy for a while. But it wasn't reciprocal, and she couldn't take a hint."

"Did she have feelings for you?" Alan asked gently.

"Maybe. I don't know." Sarah shifted in her seat. "I didn't see her that way. I made that clear after I..." She trailed off, looking away.

"After you what?" Claire pressed.

AGATHA FROST

Sarah sighed. "After I kissed her on New Year's Eve. We were at a party, we danced, we drank. Her wife wasn't around, and I kissed her at midnight. I told her the next day it was just the tequila. That's when she started acting strange with me. Not long after, the accusations about me stealing started flying around the garden centre. I think she was angry that I rejected her advances and wanted revenge."

Claire's pulse quickened at this new information. She recalled Tom mentioning that Nigella had personal reasons for disliking Sarah. Perhaps this explained the tension she'd observed. Sarah bit her lip, her eyes on her wristwatch, and Claire sensed they had little time left.

"Is there anything else you'd like to tell us?" Alan asked, his voice soft. "Anything you think might help us figure out what happened to Nigella?"

"I need to get on with my job search," Sarah said, her voice small. "I won't be able to claim benefits for weeks because I quit, so I can't stay out of work for long. I'm already behind on rent, and if I don't find something soon, I—"

"If you answer my previous question, I can promise to get you a job interview," Alan said, reaching into his pocket for a small pink business card. "The work is hard, but the pay is fair."

He slid the card across the table, and Sarah snatched it

up. Her brows furrowed as she read the name on the logo.

"Janet's Angels?" she said. "As in the Janet who I—?" She paused and said, "The Janet who accused me of stealing her purse?"

"You're a young mum of two who, until yesterday, had a full-time job, and your flat is still immaculate," Alan said, gesturing around the place. Claire looked around; she hadn't noticed how neat everything was before, but he was right. It put her own flat—with its leftover pizza boxes and scattered clothes—to shame. "If I know my wife, she won't hold a grudge if you know your way around a cleaning cupboard. So, the question?"

Sarah spun the card between two fingers before pocketing it in her hoodie.

"Nigella thought Bernard wanted her gone from the garden centre," she said, standing up. "He put her rent up for that little patch to where she was barely making any profit from the bees, even with all the demand she had for her honey. That's all she told me. Now, if you don't mind."

"We've already taken up enough of your time," Alan said, reaching for the nearest door. "Is this the way we came in—"

Alan opened the door to a small storage cupboard before shutting it quickly. Bowing in embarrassment, he shuffled toward the actual exit. Sarah locked the door behind them, and they set off back towards the lifts. His embarrassed smile vanished, his eyes narrowing as he slipped into his thoughts.

"The cupboard wasn't an accident, was it?" Claire said, catching his wry smile. "Was it filled with beekeeping equipment?"

"No," he said, jabbing the lift button with the tip of his cane. "But there was an industrial-sized bag of coffee beans in there. I could smell them, which is why I looked."

"She made a pot of tea."

"Well observed, little one."

"And she said 'I' before she said 'she' when talking about Mum's purse," Claire thought aloud as the lift doors slid open. "So, it's safe to say she's the thief?"

"Unfortunately, I think she took your mother's purse and panicked when Janet called the police. She might also have been stealing coffee beans from the café. However, the beekeeping equipment listings have yet to sell, so unless they're stashed somewhere else in that tiny flat, assuming she stole everything is not fair."

"Mum's going to flip that you gave her a business card."

"Sarah has to have the courage to call first," Alan said as the lift carried them back to the ground floor. "I'll speak with your mother. Regardless, Sarah's still a young mum who needs work and is young enough for a second chance. Good catch on the pronoun slip-up. Did you notice the other one?"

Claire scanned the conversation in her mind but she hadn't picked up on another one. She shook her head as the doors opened to the harsh morning light. Alan continued to the car, but Claire hung back in the shadow of the tower block as her phone vibrated in her back pocket. She pulled it out to read a text message:

SALLY

Dress like you can afford a £270,000 mortgage and meet me on the corner of Wordsworth Avenue at half-past three.

"Given the context of how she told the New Year's Eve story," Alan continued when Claire climbed into the passenger seat, "Sarah made it sound as though Nigella was the clingy one, correct?"

"That's what it sounded like to me."

"And yet she didn't say 'she kissed me,' as in Nigella kissed her; she said 'I kissed her,' as in Sarah kissed Nigella, and she said that twice." They climbed into the car, and once inside, Alan exhaled deeply. "The photo of the two of them by the bee shed was one I hung up for my own reference, but it was a snapshot of a longer video that Bernard supplied me with when he asked me to investigate Sarah. The moment I printed was seconds before the two of them kissed again, and Sarah was most certainly the one to initiate the kiss. Nigella walked away, leaving Sarah to chase after her."

"So, Sarah is a liar?" Claire said, pondering how this revelation fit into the bigger picture. "We can't trust anything she said."

"Lies mixed with truths, I imagine. But there's something else. That video was taken just a week before Nigella died," Alan said, sighing as he started the engine. "Before Nigella's death, the kiss didn't hold much significance, but now it's taken on a different context. As of right now, we can't rule out the young thief. Shall we head back to the shop, little one?"

A LOVER OF CASUAL AND COMFORTABLE OUTFITS, CLAIRE dug out the smartest blazer and trousers she owned from the back of her wardrobe. She ripped off the tags and was glad to have a use for the stuffy clothes her mother had bought her two Christmases ago. After changing, she fed the cats before joining Damon in the modestly busy shop, where he was transferring candles from a cardboard box to the central display.

"This is the last of the wildflowers," Damon said, standing back to take in the thin display. "So much for making enough to last the rest of the month. What's the plan when they've all sold, boss? Oh, you look… different."

Claire tugged at her slightly too small jacket, certain her mother had chosen an 'aspirational' size for her. "Do I look like someone who can afford a mortgage?"

"Maybe someone who sells mortgages?"

"Close enough."

"You and Ryan are thinking of buying somewhere together? You've kept that quiet."

"Not quite." Claire kicked the empty cardboard box into the back room before grabbing her keys. "Are you okay to close up if I'm not back in time?"

"Always."

Claire headed out while checking the location of Wordsworth Avenue on her phone. She was relieved to see it was close to Northash Primary School. With hurried steps, she trekked up the incline of Starfall Park and emerged at Upper Northash before turning left and hurrying across the top road towards the outskirts.

Claire arrived at Northash Primary School, weaving through clusters of other parents around the gates. She spotted Amelia and Hugo mingling in the playground, clad in red jumpers and white polo shirts—the same uniform Claire and Ryan had worn. Amelia wasted no time teasing Claire about her 'mortgage makeover,' declaring that she resembled the school receptionist.

Hugo grinned, suggesting she looked more like a spy about to embark on a secret mission.

Claire laughed and whispered, "Fancy joining me on a little mission, agents?"

Their eyes sparkled with curiosity, and they set off towards Wordsworth Avenue. On their walk, Claire asked about their day at school. Hugo puffed out his chest and announced he'd received top marks in his maths test. Rolling her eyes, Amelia pointed out that she'd stained purple paint on her uniform during her art lesson. As they rounded the corner onto Wordsworth Avenue, Claire assured her they'd try to wash it back at the flat. The tree-lined street boasted medium-sized detached houses, private driveways, and garages. The street was mostly tranquil, except for a few children returning home from school.

Given the mortgage price, it was the kind of street Claire could only ever dream of living on.

They reached the corner where Sally was waiting, dressed in an outfit almost matching Claire's.

"Nice touch," Sally said, nodding at the children. "It's a big family home."

"What's the mission?" Hugo whispered. "Are we catching the poisoner?"

"Your mission, if you choose to accept it," Claire whispered, following Sally through the gate, "is to be as well-behaved as possible."

"It's just gone up to *three* milkshakes," Amelia said.

Sally knocked on the vivid red door, and after a moment, it swung open to reveal an attractive woman, close to fifty, with auburn hair. A sweet cloud of perfume swirled around her, and although a weary look resided in her eyes, she otherwise showed no outward signs of recent bereavement.

"Hi, Fiona," Sally greeted her cheerfully. "I know we're a little early, but is it alright to come in and get this viewing underway?"

Fiona's eyes darted over Claire and the children with a mixture of curiosity and appraisal. "Absolutely. Please, come in."

As they followed Fiona into the open-plan interior, Claire glanced around, taking note of the high ceilings and modern furnishings.

"Posh place," Amelia remarked.

"There's a big garden out the back," Fiona pointed out with a manicured hand. "Complete with a tree house."

"Tree house?" Amelia and Hugo replied in unison.

The children took it upon themselves to run ahead to check out the back garden, leaving Sally and Claire in the hallway. Claire wasn't sure how she would slip in questions about Fiona's ex without giving herself away.

"All recently redecorated," Fiona offered, her smile unwavering. "I must say, I'm surprised to have a viewing so soon. The sign hasn't been put up outside yet."

"That's the sort of service we offer at Smith and Smith Estate Agents," Sally said, pulling her phone from her jacket pocket. "Are you okay to show Miss Harris around the downstairs, Fiona? I have to take this call."

"Of course," Fiona said. "Please, Miss Harris, this way."

Claire followed Fiona into the glossy kitchen, exchanging pleasant small talk about the sunny spring weather as she pointed out features like the 'charming bay windows' and 'spacious open floor plan.' Claire did her best to seem enthused as she wandered through each tidy room, discreetly glancing at framed photos and scanning for any clues that might shed light on the state of Nigella and Fiona's relationship prior to the murder.

In the living room, her eyes landed on a large photograph from their wedding day displayed prominently on the fireplace mantel. It was the same one Damon had shown her online. The two women glowed joyfully, their arms wrapped around each other in white dresses and floral crowns. She noticed Fiona had made no effort to hide or remove it.

Thinking about her father's tactful approach with Sarah earlier—holding back most of what he knew—Claire decided to seize the opportunity right before her.

"I'm so sorry for your loss," Claire said, not taking her eyes off the picture. "I had no idea you were Nigella's wife."

"Oh, thank you," Fiona said, glancing at the photo. A

flash of sadness crossed her delicate features before she quickly masked it with a polite smile. "We've been separated for most of this year. The estate agent suggested I keep some personal photos out to help warm the place up a little. Truth be told, I haven't been able to bring myself to take it down." She paused, turning to Claire. "How did you know Nigella?"

"I have a little candle shop in town. I bought some wax from her."

"I think I've walked past it a few times," Fiona said, busying herself with rearranging a stack of decorative books on the coffee table. "Those bloody bees. She put them before everything. I—" She cleared her throat, shaking her head. "I'm sorry; that's not why you're here."

"It's fine," Claire said quickly, not wanting the thread to slip away. "This can't be easy for you, even if you were separated."

Fiona smiled. "You're right… it's not been easy. I put on a brave face because I don't know what else to do. I've spent months trying to reach a divorce settlement so we can be out of each other's lives, and now that she is out of my life, it doesn't quite feel real. Have you ever been divorced?"

"Never been married," Claire admitted. "But my boyfriend, and best friend"—she left off the friend was Sally, pacing around the front garden with her phone to her ear— "have both gone through tricky divorces, so I've seen the fight from the outside."

"Then you'll know how fraught things can get," Fiona said, looking around the living room before her eyes landed on the wedding portrait. "She was trying to fight me for half of this place, even though I was the one who saved up the deposit and paid the mortgage every month. She threw her life savings and every penny she made into her hobby. I thought we'd start a family here, start a life, but I was never first to her. When I told her it was me or the bees, I never expected she wouldn't choose her wife." She shook her head, schooling her features back into a neutral mask. "Are you okay to poke around upstairs on your own? I need some fresh air."

"Of course."

"You're welcome to view every room except the one with the closed door. My brother is staying with me and isn't feeling too well."

Fiona marched through the dining room and out into the garden through the patio doors. Given how Nigella had first brought up her soon-to-be ex-wife, Claire hadn't expected them to be on great terms, but she also hadn't expected their split to revolve around beekeeping. After Sarah's New Year's Eve party admission that morning, she'd half-expected infidelity to be the reason for the break-up. If Fiona was being truthful, it didn't sound like she'd wanted the marriage to end, despite her ultimatum.

Claire watched as Amelia and Hugo dashed towards the treehouse, their earlier mission of spying apparently forgotten in the promise of adventure. She couldn't help but smile at their unrestrained enthusiasm despite the lingering unease this viewing had stirred within her. Glancing back through the glass doors, she could see Fiona standing with her arms folded across her chest, gazing out across the back garden with a pensive expression. Claire hesitated, wondering if she should return and offer some words of comfort. With a resigned sigh, she turned and headed for the stairs.

Once upstairs, Claire poked her head into what was clearly the master suite, taking in the king-size bed with its plush ivory duvet and the en-suite bathroom fitted with both a shower and an elaborate Jacuzzi tub. She tried to picture Nigella and Fiona spending evenings curled up together in that bed, limbs entwined, whispering sweet nothings. But the image felt hollow. This house may have been their marital home, but it was clear from Fiona's account that there had been little joy recently.

Next, she ventured into an empty room that might have been an office, with empty shelves waiting to be filled with files, books, and trinkets. Yet its soft pastel colour scheme seemed too gentle for a workplace.

Claire's heart tugged as she realised it was a space that could have easily transformed into a nursery—a silent testament to plans and dreams unfulfilled.

As she approached the closed bedroom door, she could hear the canned laughter and cheerful music of a daytime quiz show filtering through. Fiona's brother, she presumed. Whoever he was, he clearly had no qualms about making himself at home in the house his sister was trying to sell.

Claire opened the next door and was hit by a wall of steam. She was met by the surprised eyes of a tall man, half-covered with a towel, his face adorned with shaving foam as he stood in front of a bathroom mirror. He looked at her quizzically, as if mentally flipping through a Rolodex of faces to place her.

"Oh—I'm sorry!" Claire stuttered, retreating. "I'm here for the house viewing."

"No harm done," he said, closing the door with his shaving foam hidden hands without another word.

Feeling a little embarrassed by the intrusion, Claire returned downstairs and met Sally in the hallway, the estate agent's phone back in her pocket.

"Got everything you need?" she asked. "I've got a legitimate viewing in about twenty minutes."

"Think I've seen all I can," Claire said. "Especially after walking in on Fiona's brother fresh out of the shower."

"Ah, I should have warned you. That would be Tom."

Claire's thoughts flew back to that towering figure in the beekeeping suit. She hadn't seen his face, but she'd heard his voice. She tried to connect the voice in her memory with the three words still fresh in her mind, but she couldn't be sure.

"Tom who?"

Sally shrugged. "Not sure."

After thanking Sally for getting her a conversation with Fiona, as brief as it was, Claire gathered Amelia and Hugo from the garden, who were bursting with energy after their adventure in the treehouse.

"I've only ever seen them in films," Hugo exclaimed as they approached the front garden gate. "Do you think we'll ever live somewhere with a treehouse? Our back garden doesn't even have plants."

"One day," Amelia assured him. "I'll make sure of it. How did your snooping go, Claire? Find any evidence?"

"I'm not sure."

"Not much of a spy, are you?" Amelia said. "We did a better job outside."

"We only overheard her on the phone," Hugo corrected. "Dad said we shouldn't listen to people when they're on the phone."

"Well, Dad isn't here, is he?" Amelia replied as though that settled it.

"Overheard who?" Claire asked as they set off down the street. "Sally?"

"No, the crying woman," Amelia said. "She was talking to someone. Sounded important."

"What did she say?"

"She said she's leaving the country as soon as the house sells," Hugo said. "Are you going to buy her house, Claire?"

"No," Claire replied, ruffling his hair. "It's a little out of my price range, but good work, kids. How about we knock one of those milkshakes off my bill on our way back to the shop?"

Claire felt her heartbeat quicken as they walked toward the top entrance of Starfall Park. The timing for Fiona selling her house was bad enough, but leaving the country too? And what had Fiona said about Nigella wanting half of the house? If the two had been battling about how to split their assets in the divorce, Fiona had just conveniently walked away with everything.

Back at the shop with Amelia and Hugo—along with the cats and their chocolate milkshakes in the upstairs flat—Claire and Damon leaned against the counter, peering at the shop's tablet as they scrolled through Fiona's Facebook profile again.

"She's the deputy head at Moorhead High School," Damon pointed out after a slurp of his banana shake. "Would someone with a cushy job like that sell up and flee the country unless they felt they had to?"

"Not if I lived somewhere like that," Claire said.

"Found it," Damon said, tapping the screen. "Before they married in 2012, Fiona went by Middleton, which means her brother is Tom Middleton."

Pulling off the lid of her strawberry milkshake to stir the thick liquid with her deteriorating paper straw, Claire wondered if there was any significance to the fact that Nigella's business partner was also her widow's brother. And why was he hiding out at his sister's house when the police couldn't reach him?

CHAPTER SEVEN

*C*laire took a sip of her fresh coffee as she gazed out of the kitchen window at the cul-de-sac that evening. The setting sun cast a fuzzy glow across the back garden, where Hugo and Amelia were immersed in their own worlds. Hugo lay on his stomach in the grass, his brow furrowed in concentration as he played on his game console. Amelia sat cross-legged under the oak tree by the shed, her tongue poking out of the corner of her mouth as she added the finishing touches to a sketch in her drawing pad.

The opening bars of ABBA's 'Dancing Queen' floated in from the living room, followed by Janet's indignant yelp. "Alan! I'm trying to vacuum."

"There's always time for a dance, my love," Alan

replied. "Don't you remember showing everyone how it's done with this one at our wedding?"

Chuckling to herself as she pictured her father trying to twirl her mother around the room, Claire carried her coffee into the back garden and towards the fence separating her parents' garden from the house next door. Ryan was leaning against the fence, staring into his old childhood garden.

"Penny for your thoughts?" Claire asked, coming up beside him.

Ryan turned, giving her a soft smile. "Just thinking. We had a lot of good times living here, didn't we?"

"We really did." Nostalgia washed over Claire as she thought back to endless summer days playing in these back gardens. "I half expect your mum to come to the back door, covered in paint, asking what we're staring at."

Ryan chuckled. "Not just me then?" He turned back to the children, and his expression grew pensive. "The kids seem happy here at the cul-de-sac. They were in a weird mood last night after seeing that fancy house with the treehouse. Hugo said she wished they had a bigger garden she could really run around in." He let out a long sigh, his shoulders slumping. "I'm trying my best for them. I really am. But no matter how I juggle my budget, your Uncle Pat's old place is eating up everything. I hate the thought that I had a better childhood than they're having."

Claire set her coffee down on a rock and reached over to squeeze his hand. "The childhood they deserve is one filled with love. And they have that in spades. You're a great dad, Ryan. A big garden and a treehouse would be the cherry on top, but a cherry is just a cherry."

He smiled, squeezing her hand in return. "I suppose you're right. When I first moved back here after I left Spain, I just had this image of what a childhood in Northash would be like for them, and I've realised that version is further out of reach than I'd dreamt it would be."

"You've come a long way since you returned," Claire said, resting her head on his shoulder. "You were living in the B&B for months, and you clawed your way out of there, and—"

"No, you're right," Ryan interrupted with a little laugh. "I'm just being silly. Rough day at work, that's all. I plucked up the courage to ask my boss for that manager promotion, and he seemed surprised that I thought I was an option."

"Oh, Ryan. I'm sorry."

"But you were right," he continued, leaning back on the fence. "I never saw myself ending up working in a gym, but I am good at it. People do enjoy my classes, and I'm always the first in and the last out." He glanced at Claire, a smile tugging at his lips. "I looked online at other gyms advertising more senior positions with better pay. There's a small place in Burnley that's looking for a manager."

"Burnley?" Claire echoed, biting back the comment that it was at least a forty-minute drive away. "You're thinking of moving?"

"Property prices are much cheaper there," he said with a shrug. "I still wouldn't be able to afford anything right now, but I'd get there a lot quicker."

Claire hesitated, wanting to offer reassurance but unsure of what to say. She still vividly remembered the day Ryan had moved to Spain all those years ago, heartbroken at losing her best friend and leaving her behind in the cul-de-sac. The thought of him leaving again made her feel sick.

"I'm just thinking out loud," he said before pulling her close to kiss her forehead tenderly. "I should get the kids home to get ready for bed. See you tomorrow?"

Claire nodded, wanting to ask him to stay over for another night. He'd already stayed two nights in a row, and they'd never made it to three. With a final squeeze of her hand, he headed over to collect Amelia and Hugo. Claire watched as the little family made their way down the garden path, Ryan ruffling the children's hair and making them giggle. It felt strange not to be following behind.

After they had disappeared from view, she collected her coffee cup and headed inside, finding DI

Ramsbottom in the sitting room. A half-eaten slice of Victoria sponge sat on a plate in front of him, while her dad poured them both fresh cups of tea.

"Ah, Claire, you're just in time," Alan said. "Harry's got an update on the case."

"Just a small one," Ramsbottom said through a mouthful of cake. He dabbed at his mouth with a napkin. "Excellent baking, as always, Janet."

"Shop-bought," she said, though she smiled all the same. "M&S's finest range. Don't have much time for baking these days. Quite moist, wouldn't you say?"

Claire perched next to her mother on the sofa and noticed a jar of honey on the coffee table. She was about to ask if another jar had shown up when she noticed the 'MIND YOUR BEESWAX, BUSYBODY!' label hanging from the red ribbon.

"We tested it every which way in the lab, and no poison detected at all," Ramsbottom told her. "Just your standard wildflower honey. We did have to extract a fair-sized sample to cover all our bases. Hope you don't mind it coming back a little emptier. But it's safe to use it on your porridge, or whatever it is you do with honey. I've always been more of a fan of golden syrup, myself."

Claire turned the honey jar over in her hands. The liquid inside was far runnier than the honey jar Nigella had given her in exchange for the candles. She made a mental note to compare the two, though she wasn't sure it meant anything.

Oblivious to her scrutiny of the honey, Ramsbottom continued, "I'm afraid we've rather hit a dead end with the case. Unless something new comes to light, I may have to close this case as an accidental poisoning, given that foxglove was all over the place."

"Foxglove?" Claire asked, putting the jar back on the table. "Was that the poison used?"

"I have some of the pink variety in the garden," Alan said, motioning about the height of Hugo. "They can grow quite big. Lovely things to look at."

"They contain something called 'cardiac glycosides,' you see," Ramsbottom mumbled through another mouthful, his unsure pronunciation suggesting he'd only recently learned the term. "They're organic compounds that increase the force of the heart and decrease its rate of contractions. Quite handy when used in medications for heart failure and arrhythmias, but when used incorrectly... drowsiness, unsteadiness, seizures, and, in Nigella's case, death. It was her heart that gave out in the end."

"And you think she somehow did this to herself?" Janet asked bluntly. "Seems far-fetched to me, Harry."

"Perhaps she foraged some and ate it, thinking it was something else?" he suggested. "You know what those outdoor types are like. Maybe one of the flowers fell into her tea, and she didn't notice?"

"Her tea," Claire repeated, squinting at the honey jar. "She was sipping tea when I was talking to her by the hives. She seemed mostly fine then, but when I saw her a little later in the café, she was drowsy and unsteady. She dropped her tea on the floor. I noticed some strange stuff in the puddle when Sarah was mopping it up."

"Strange stuff?" Ramsbottom perked up. "Why didn't you mention that before?"

"Is there a way to test the floors?" Claire suggested, looking at her father rather than the DI.

"Perhaps? Depends how well the floors have been cleaned since," he said.

"They weren't that clean when I was there," Janet said, in a disapproving manner. "The whole place could have done with a deep clean, but that's just me."

"Something to look into," Ramsbottom said, scribbling the note on his pad. "What about your meeting with Fiona, Claire? Your father called to tell us Tom was staying there, and we've since spoken to him."

"What's Tom got to say for himself?" Claire asked. "Why was he hiding?"

"Claims not to have been," Ramsbottom admitted, reaching for the plate he'd already cleared before looping his fingers together. "Claims he didn't know Nigella had been murdered and was staying with his sister to save money. Says his relationship with Nigella was purely business—more a favour to Fiona than anything."

Claire thought back to that argument; they'd seemed close enough then.

"That's not quite true," Janet said on Claire's behalf. "The pair of them were round here that night, remember, Alan? When you were drinking whisky in the shed? Seemed friendly to me."

"Yes, they did seem to get on quite well," Alan agreed, nodding. "Though Tom didn't seem to know the first thing about beekeeping, and they did start bickering about the ethics of his business proposals for the company."

"Who's looking after the bees?" Claire asked.

"They're being cared for by some apprentice who worked with Nigella sometimes," Ramsbottom recalled. "Hayley, I think she's called. Lovely lass. Seems she'll keep the operation running until Tom figures out what to do next. He's now the sole owner, but, like Alan said, he doesn't know much about how to run the business." He finished his tea and stood, brushing crumbs from his tweed jacket. "Well, I'd best be off. There's a pie at The Park Inn with my name on it. Thanks again for the hospitality. Any new developments, you'll be the first to know."

"I'll walk you to the door," Alan said.

As soon as Ramsbottom was out of the sitting room,

Claire's thoughts whirred into action. Foxglove. A poisonous plant that her dad had in their garden and was all over the garden centre. That strange substance she saw on the café floor after Nigella spilled her tea. Tom and his lack of knowledge in beekeeping, despite co-owning a company dedicated to it. There were too many elements that didn't quite fit together, yet Claire had an itch she couldn't quite scratch—a feeling that all these puzzle pieces were part of the same puzzle that would lead them to uncovering the truth of what happened to Nigella.

"That man is a total pig," Janet muttered to herself as she went about cleaning up the remains of the feast. "I put out an entire Victoria sponge for us to share, and he polished the whole thing off like it was a snack. If he focused on the case as much as his stomach, he'd have solved it by—"

The house phone rang off in the hall, and Janet went off muttering, no doubt about 'who calls at this time on a Sunday', leaving Claire to finish clearing the sitting room. She stacked the plates and cutlery by the sink and glanced through the window as the sun dipped below the horizon. Her father had walked around the side of the house and was on his way to the shed. She wasn't about to miss his debriefing.

Claire walked down the garden path, her eyes set on the shed. But as she drew closer, a wave of unease swept through her when her father abruptly stopped. The shed door hung slightly open, and inside, the dim bulb swayed, throwing unsettling shadows across the walls. Alan turned and held out an arm to stop her from advancing any further.

"Stay here, Claire," he said, his face serious. "It's my shed to check."

With cautious steps, Alan approached the shed, with Claire right behind him. As he pushed the door open with the end of the cane, the exposed light bulb distorted the shadows inside, making it difficult to see if anyone was there. The shed appeared empty at first glance, but the bulb wasn't swinging for no reason.

"Better not let your mother see this mess," he whispered, and Claire admired his levity. "She'll insist on throwing everything out."

The place had been ransacked. Drawers were pulled open. Bags of potting soil lay upended. The investigation board, with all its meticulously gathered notes and clues about the stolen items, destroyed. Claire turned to her upturned plant pot, letting out a sigh of relief for the small mercy that it remained intact—exactly where it had been for as long as she could remember.

"They must have been in here minutes ago," Claire said, standing on her tiptoes to steady the swaying bulb. "We could check the fields."

"In the dark?" He shook his head, staring at something

on his potting desk. "They could have gone in any direction, but it was nice of them to leave us a little present."

On the potting desk, another jar of honey—identical to the one that had been tested earlier—glowed under the exposed light bulb. And there was another note attached to it. The words sent a chill down Claire's spine. The note read, 'I WILL STING...'

"This is more than just a warning, Claire. Whoever did this wanted to show their ability to evade us right under our noses. The leading DI on the case was inside the house enjoying tea and cakes while this happened."

Claire's heart pounded in her chest. "What do we do, Dad?"

Alan's expression hardened, his determination shining through. "We take this threat seriously. We double down on our efforts to uncover the truth before they strike again. We can't afford to underestimate our adversary. We need to be vigilant, or else... well... we'll feel their sting."

CHAPTER EIGHT

*M*eadowview Garden Centre greeted them on a cloudy Saturday morning, its car park's puddles reflecting the grey sky. To counter the unexpected spring chill, Claire adjusted the collar of her faded denim jacket while trailing her father through the main entrance. Amid shelves adorned with terracotta pots, garden tools, and an array of gloves, her father maintained an engaging, ongoing conversation.

"I wish things would go back to normal here," he whispered as they headed through the entrance. "Never thought I'd return to work, but this place is quite ideal for me. I get to potter about doing what I love, and it gets me out and about while your mother's running around the county giving everything a spit and polish."

Claire's fingers tightened around the strap of her

handbag as her eyes darted around the garden centre. Every customer, every shelf, held a potential clue. She couldn't shake the uneasy feeling that someone was watching them, like a shadow lurking just beyond her vision. The recent jar incidents only deepened her sense of unease.

Reaching the end of the gardening tools aisle, Claire let her father's voice fade into background noise. She studied the morning customers milling about. Most seemed focused on their shopping, but she couldn't shake the prickly feeling at the back of her neck that someone was watching them. She'd felt it while walking home the previous night and when opening her shop earlier that morning.

"Business as usual, remember?" Alan whispered, his eyes scanning the shelves. "We don't want to let on that we're scared, or else whoever left that little 'present' will think they've won. Looks like they're running low on trowels. I should restock them. Don't want customers leaving empty-handed. I'll go find Bernard to get the key to the stockroom. This time of morning, he's usually in his office."

Alan scurried off, leaving Claire to linger by the tools. She looked up at the cameras covering the aisle, feeling a little safer. At least if Nigella's murderer turned up to stab a gardening fork through their midsection, her parents would know who did it. Morbid as her thoughts were, seeing the cameras gave her an idea. A young lad in the same green polo as her father dropped off a box of trowels before Alan returned.

"There are cameras all over this aisle," Claire pointed out. "If tools were being taken, surely the culprit would've been seen?"

"A thought I had myself," Alan agreed, ripping open the box. "Bernard gave me some clips of the aisle, but none of the stolen items were taken from the shop floor. They must've been taken between delivery and stocking the shelves. The delivered boxes go into the storeroom, and only Bernard has a key. As it stands, there's no way to know if the stolen items have anything to do with Nigella's death." After sliding the first trowel onto the empty rack, he nodded towards the closed café, where forensic officers were examining the scene. "Looks like they're taking your poisoned-tea theory seriously."

"At least they're doing something," Claire said, sliding a silver trowel next to its blue counterpart. "I've been thinking about whether the stolen items could be connected to Nigella. Sarah has kissed her at least twice, but Nigella suspected Sarah of the thefts. What if Sarah kissed Nigella to throw her off the scent?"

"A distraction?" Alan pondered. "And I assume the logical conclusion of your theory is that Sarah poisoned Nigella to keep her thievery a secret once and for all?"

Claire nodded, recalling how the theory had spun

around in her mind during last night's bath, accompanied by one of the few wildflower-scented candles she'd reserved for herself. It was a shame they'd sold out so quickly; the formula was one of her favourites.

"Sarah had those coffee beans in her cupboard," Claire reminded him. "If she's as skilled a thief as she'd need to be to cover her tracks, who's saying she didn't steal the key to the storeroom too? She could have her own copy."

Her father rubbed his forehead, eyes narrowing in thought. "You have a point. It's quite convincing when you put it like that. But there are other suspects to consider. I spoke briefly with Bernard just now; he's acting as if everything is business as usual. He even mentioned the opportunity to sell your candles here again. Have you given it any more thought?"

"None at all," Claire admitted. "I've felt so distracted. I should be focusing on the shop, but…"

"You're preoccupied," Alan said, patting her shoulder. "I know that feeling all too well, which is why we should resolve this sooner rather than later. Who are our other suspects?"

"What about Fiona and Tom?" Claire suggested. "Both had obvious connections to Nigella. You said yourself that Tom seemed eager to push Nigella into expanding the business. And Fiona told me that Nigella wanted to take half of everything in the divorce."

"And now Fiona gets to walk away without dividing

any assets," Alan agreed, nodding carefully as he set off, kicking the empty box along the aisle with his good foot. "Tom, Bernard, and Sarah were all here the day Nigella was poisoned, but was Fiona?"

"Nigella said that Fiona called her," Claire said. "She could have visited as well to slip the poison into her tea."

Before Alan could respond, his gaze fixed on something over Claire's shoulder. "Speaking of which, look who has just arrived."

Claire turned to see Tom stepping out of a mud-splattered Land Rover in the car park. After locking the vehicle, he strode towards the garden centre entrance, carrying a large box held in place with thick gardening gloves.

"You wanted to speak with him again about the case," Alan said. "Here's your chance."

While her father continued his box-kicking shuffle back to the stockroom, Claire headed for the rear of the garden centre. She wove between displays of flowerpots and trellises until she reached the fenced-off area housing the beehives.

The buzz of activity greeted her as she approached the small wooden structures. Claire smiled sadly, reminded of her conversations with Nigella. The beekeeper had always been so passionate about her work, her eyes lighting up when she spoke about the hive.

Although Nigella had been dead only a few days, her vibrant presence already felt like a distant memory.

In her place stood Tom, garbed in the white, hooded beekeeper suit Claire had first seen him wear. The box he'd brought inside sat open next to him, revealing what looked like pieces of a new hive ready to be assembled. Claire also noticed a young woman with long, golden hair and a nose ring that glinted as she inspected frames loaded with honeycomb and bees.

"Hello there," Claire called, stopping a few metres away from the cloud of bees surrounding Hayley as she worked. "I'm Claire. I used to buy wax from Nigella for my candles."

Hayley glanced up, a hint of caution in her gaze that disappeared as she offered a faint smile.

"Ah, you're the candle lady, aren't you?" she replied. "I'm Hayley, and I'm sorry to be the bearer of bad news, but—"

"Claire knows," Tom interjected, setting down the hive piece he was examining and strolling over. "Her father works here part-time. Nice chap. You were here that morning, weren't you? Behind that tree?"

Claire glanced at the tree behind which she'd eavesdropped. "I was."

"Well, it's good to see you again," he said, an odd note in his voice. Claire met his stare, half-expecting him to mention the awkward incident when he'd walked in on her in Fiona's bathroom, but he said nothing. Behind the mesh screen hiding his freshly shaven face, he was quite handsome.

"We have a batch of wax ready if you're interested," he continued. "We'll have even more soon, now that we're expanding operations."

At this, Hayley looked up from her work. "Nigella always wanted to keep things small, you know," she said, her voice tinged with defensiveness. "She said it was easier to maintain ethical practices that way."

Tom rolled his eyes. "That's not realistic if we want to keep this space. Bernard increased the rent, so we have to ramp up production. That's just business, Hayley. With you in charge, I'm sure you'll manage just as ethically, even with a few extra hives."

Claire sensed an opportunity to probe gently for information. "Speaking of Bernard, I heard Nigella thought he wanted her gone from the garden centre, hence the rent hike. Is that true?"

Tom eyed her with sudden suspicion. "What's it to you?"

"Oh, just being nosy, I suppose," Claire replied with a casual shrug. "Runs in the family. My dad used to be a detective inspector."

After a pause, Hayley spoke again. "I remember Nigella saying Bernard wanted her to sell honey here. She never had many jars left after selling to her regulars.

That's how we met. Her local pollen based honey really helped with my hay fever. She was so inspiring... I miss her already."

"We all miss Nigella, of course. She was like family," Tom said, touching Hayley's shoulder gently. "Why don't you get back to the new hive frames? I'll box up some wax for Claire."

Grateful for the diversion, Hayley refocused on the bees. Tom faced Claire again, his expression unreadable.

"Listen, despite our disagreements about how to run things, Nigella meant a lot to me," he stated. "If you're trying to imply anything sinister, you are way off base."

Claire tried to maintain an unreadable expression in return. "Just asking questions, that's all."

He moved to the nearby shed and rummaged around. After a moment, he returned with a large tray filled with wax bricks wrapped in parchment paper.

"Enough for plenty of candles, I'd say," he said. "Call it ten percent off this batch, considering you're our only wax customer for the time being. If you know of any other crafty people, feel free to send them our way, and I'll keep the discount going."

He held out the tray, which Claire accepted after a brief hesitation. She could feel his eyes on her as she bid them both goodbye and retreated from the beekeeping area, her mind spinning.

There was tension simmering below the surface

between Tom and Hayley regarding the future of the beekeeping business. Bernard seemed intent on using his position as the owner to force operations to expand for higher profits, despite Nigella's wishes.

So lost in thought, Claire nearly collided with Bernard himself as she rounded a corner. The man sidestepped her deftly, clutching a tray containing two cups of tea. The corners of his mouth turned upward into a cheek-creasing grin.

"Claire! Just who I wanted to see," he exclaimed. "Have you thought any more about selling your candles here? You'd make a pretty penny, I guarantee it."

"I'm afraid I haven't."

"Oh, come on, Claire," he said, leaning in. "One local small business to another, eh? Let's help each other out here. I'd rather buy from an artisan creator like you than be forced to buy the generic stuff from Warton Candle Factory. What's there even to think about?"

Before she could respond, a flash of movement behind Bernard caught her eye. Peering past him, Claire spotted a familiar blonde pixie crop through the open door of a room next to the sectioned-off café. The former waitress was sitting at a desk, digging at something in her nails.

Glancing back at Bernard, Claire noticed his lips thin in displeasure before he pasted the smile back on.

"Sarah's come begging for her old job back, would you believe?" he murmured, leaning closer to Claire.

"Between you and me, I might take her on again but dock her pay back down to minimum wage. Make her think twice about stealing from under my nose, won't it?"

Claire stared at him wordlessly. The business card he'd given her during their first meeting burned a deep hole in her back pocket. Without a word, she dug it out and dropped it onto the tray between the two teacups.

"I've thought about it," she said. "You'll have to find another candle supplier for your venture."

"Whatever. I'm sure they stink anyway," Bernard laughed to himself as he turned on his heels and carried the tray into the room. He slammed the door, and before it shut, Sarah caught Claire's eye. After their meeting yesterday and how the young mum had called the working environment 'toxic,' it surprised Claire she'd crawl back so soon.

Claire's heart raced as she practically sprinted toward the exit. Each step felt like a desperate attempt to escape the mounting weight of unanswered questions gnawing at her mind.

Lost in irritation, she almost didn't register the familiar figure standing by the seed-packet display up ahead. But then the woman glanced up from her phone conversation, and Claire realised, with a jolt, that it was Fiona.

Nigella's widow looked just as put together as she had

at the viewing yesterday afternoon. But her smile seemed tight and her posture tense as she spoke into her phone.

"The estate agent says it's the perfect time to list the house," Fiona was saying as Claire drew near, keeping her head down. "I know. I can't wait either. The quicker I can get to Portugal and close this chapter, the better."

Despite herself, Claire found she was unintentionally eavesdropping again as she lingered near a display of gardenias.

"Yes, I know how it looks, but I've got three more viewings lined up this week," Fiona continued. "Hopefully, I'll get a good offer soon. Then it's just a matter of packing up and putting Northash in the rear-view. I'll be glad to see the back of the place." There was a pause before Fiona's voice softened. "Don't worry, I'll be there with you soon enough. Yes, I love you too. Speak soon."

Fiona ended the call and dropped her phone into her bag. Hoping her much more casual vintage Spice Girls T-shirt was enough of a disguise to not jog Fiona's memory, Claire lowered her head and chose that moment to hurry out of the garden centre. Her mind was whirling.

So, Fiona was selling the house she'd shared with Nigella and moving to Portugal? She had a whole new life waiting for her there with someone she apparently loved, and the timing couldn't be worse.

Stepping out into the damp morning air, Claire's

balanced the tray of wax bricks. She reached into her bag, her fingers brushing past pens, receipts, and finally, her dad's car keys. She couldn't deny the stack of revelations she'd uncovered today, but she felt no closer to untangling the true roots of this mystery.

If anything, they felt more knotted than ever. Sarah, Tom, Bernard—they all seemed to have motives and secrets surrounding Nigella's tragic end. And now Fiona and her imminent move overseas added yet another thread.

As Claire loaded the wax into the car, she felt a swell of determination. She would get to the bottom of this, no matter what it took. The roots of this mystery plunged deep, but Claire would continue yanking them up, threats or not.

CHAPTER NINE

*A*fter sending Damon home a couple of hours early to glue himself to his gaming chair for the weekend, Claire closed the door behind Eugene, the final customer of the day. He'd been lingering for close to an hour, having heard about the honey jar threats sent to Claire and her father. He left disappointed, claiming it was because the 'limited-edition' wildflower candles were out of stock. Claire knew, though, that her reluctance to add to the café's rumour mill was the more likely reason.

Before turning off the lights, she cast her eyes over the table full of runny wildflower jars in the back room, hoping they'd be cured in time to restock the empty display on Monday. She didn't want to change the window display so soon. Without a new fragrance to launch, she'd have to dip into one of her older scents for the first time. She'd never sold out of a Star Candle so quickly. Ignoring the box of online orders still needing packing labels, Claire locked up, fed the cats in the flat upstairs, and set off for the cul-de-sac. She'd closed half an hour early, but the morning's lingering rain had scared off the shoppers long before Eugene arrived. She was too distracted to notice if anyone else would turn up on the off-chance.

Claire buttoned up her faded denim jacket and quickened her pace under one of her father's golf umbrellas. As she entered the cul-de-sac, she noticed Sally's car parked outside Mrs Beaton's house. Her old neighbour had moved into a nursing home last autumn after her mental faculties began to fade. Claire and her mother had helped clear out the hoard she'd amassed in the house—once filled with cats—but judging by the uninterested faces of the couple Sally was showing around the dated sitting room, Mrs Beaton's house wasn't going to sell anytime soon. Claire hoped she was faring as well as she had been during her last visit a few months ago.

As Claire reached her parents' house in the middle of the cul-de-sac, the door opened before she could even finish squeezing the handle down.

"Now take off your shoes," Janet instructed. "The

carpet's just been shampooed. Sarah's here about the cleaning job, so I'm putting her through her paces."

Claire followed her mother down the hallway and peeked into the sitting room. Sarah was polishing the ornaments on the mantelpiece, though there was nothing to polish. Janet would vacuum the dust from the air before it had a chance to settle if she could, but Sarah was treating them as though they were filthy anyway as she rubbed at the silver and gold frames. They shared a quick smile as she glanced at Claire.

"Wouldn't be a punishment, would it?" Claire asked as they entered the kitchen. "For the purse?"

"What do you take me for?" Janet snatched up the kettle to fill it at the sink. "I'm making her a cup of tea, aren't I? And I promised your father I'd give her a fair shot if she called. Lo-and-behold, she called."

It took guts, Claire thought. She was glad to hear Sarah hadn't accepted Bernard's lowlife offer at the garden centre earlier. It must have made calling the woman who accused her of stealing her purse a long-shot Plan B. Claire hoped to speak with her again before her mother sent her off to the attic to hand-remove every cobweb.

"Your father's in the garden," Janet said, adding a splash of milk to the tea. "If you're sticking around for dinner, I'll have to fish an emergency lasagne out of the freezer."

With that, Janet marched back to continue her interview. Claire slipped out the back door and into the garden. She found her father on his knees, ensconced under another of his umbrellas jutting from the soil. He was yanking up tall clusters of pink and purple foxglove flowers that lined the fence. Claire crouched beside him.

"Usually it's the other way around, isn't it?" Claire remarked. "Need any help?"

"Only if you've covered up," Alan said, offering her a weary smile as he brushed loose soil off his gloves. "I had a quick look at one of my old gardening books. Turns out foxglove plants, as pretty as they are, can be quite dangerous—even if you don't ingest them. The oils from the leaves can irritate the skin, leading to rashes that last for weeks. And with Amelia and Hugo coming around as often as they do, I'd hate for anything to happen to them." He tugged off his gloves and assessed his work before glancing at the shed. "I was going to call you when I'd finished up here, so your timing is spot on. I have some updates that might just change everything."

Intrigued, Claire followed him across the stepping stones to the shed and took her usual perch on the plant pot. The evidence of the previous ransacking had been cleared away, but she wasn't sure how she would have reacted if the plant pot had been smashed. Maybe her father moved it when she wasn't there, but as far as she was concerned, that plant pot had been in the same spot since she was Amelia and Hugo's age.

Alan flicked on the gas heater and settled into his swivel chair.

"I conducted a bit of undercover investigation this afternoon," Alan began in a low voice. "Bernard gave me his personal key for the storeroom when I went to restock the trowels, and it happened to have a key to his office attached. He didn't ask for his keys back straight away, and I didn't offer them like I usually do. He always has lunch meetings with suppliers on Saturday afternoons, so when he drove off, I let myself in."

"Naughty, naughty," Claire whispered, grinning. "What did you find?"

"I rifled through some of the files on his desk, and I found invoices for a recent order of a wildflower—one I think you'll be able to guess."

"The same one you were just digging up?"

"Exactly," he said, nodding gravely. "Far more than the garden centre needs for its stock. If you were right about Nigella being poisoned via her tea, it wouldn't have been as simple as dropping in a few petals. If I had to guess, the flowers would have been dried out before being ground into a powder—which, of course, I couldn't prove from the invoices alone."

"Circumstantial, right?"

"Precisely," Alan agreed, leaning in further. "He left his

laptop behind on his desk, unlocked and wide open, so I had a brief look at his emails. One of the more recent ones caught my eye. I clicked on it, and it opened up a long thread of negotiations stretching back months."

"Negotiations with whom?" Claire asked.

"A factory," Alan replied. "A factory that mass-produces honey, jars it, and slaps on any label you want for a fee."

"We used to do that at the candle factory," Claire mused. "It's called white labelling. It's quite common. Bernard mentioned the candle factory earlier when he was pressuring me to stock my candles at the garden centre. I told him to stick his offer where the sun doesn't shine, and he said he'd get some mass-produced stuff instead. And Hayley, Nigella's apprentice, said Bernard wanted Nigella to stock her honey at the garden centre but there weren't enough jars to meet demand."

Alan pulled his phone from his jacket pocket. "He's quite far along in negotiations, too. Look at this." After a few taps, he showed Claire an illustrated 'Bernard's Bees' logo. She snorted at the artist's rendering of Bernard in a beekeeping uniform, surrounded by bees.

"In emails with their in-house designer, he said he wanted the logo to look as artisan and personable as possible, all while haggling the price down for buying jars in the thousands," Alan said, tucking his phone away. "Even if they were slow to sell, he could keep them in the storeroom for years. Honey has an extremely long shelf life."

"So, with Nigella not willing to meet his demands, Bernard was preparing to ramp up commercial production to go around her instead?" Claire speculated. "Sarah said he wanted to get rid of Nigella, and Tom is trying to expand the business to pay increased rent. Do you think—"

"That Bernard gave the patch to Nigella for the sole purpose of having her supply him with honey?" Alan interjected. Claire nodded. "Only to try to force her out when she had other ideas about her production methods? Yes, that's what I've been thinking about all afternoon."

"But poisoning her seems a bit extreme, doesn't it?"

"Maybe Bernard was killing two bees with one stone?" Alan mused. "Nigella was the only beekeeper I could find producing local honey in Northash. With her out of the way, Bernard could claim his white-labelled honey is the only local option, giving him a strong motive to want her gone."

"Would be useful to know if Nigella knew about his plans," Claire said.

"Perhaps Tom would know?" Alan suggested. "I could invite him over for whisky again. He seemed to enjoy getting out of the house, which makes sense considering he's staying in his sister's guest bedroom."

"Do you know how Tom and Nigella became business partners?" Claire asked.

Alan pondered the question briefly before shrugging. "Not sure, really."

"I don't think Tom will be all that forthcoming," Claire said, "but there's someone else who might be. I met Nigella's apprentice today, and she seemed—"

"Alan! Claire!" Janet's voice interrupted them, tinged with urgency. "I need help!"

Claire exchanged a puzzled glance with her father before they hurried back into the garden. Janet stood on the patio, shielding her eyes as she peered through the rain. It wouldn't be the first cleaning emergency that had driven her to raise her voice, but the worry on her face suggested something far more serious had happened.

"It's Sarah," Janet said, hurrying back inside. "One moment we were talking about when she could get started, the next she turned as white as a sheet and collapsed right out of her chair onto the floor. I've never seen anything like it. She's barely breathing."

Dread pooled in Claire's stomach as she dashed down the hallway to the sitting room. Sarah lay crumpled on the floor, her skin chalky, her breaths coming in weak, sporadic gasps. Alan rolled Sarah onto her side and into the recovery position while Janet phoned for an ambulance in the hallway.

Feeling as if time had ground to a halt and sensing her

own uselessness, Claire gazed down at Sarah's limp form. She feared she already knew what had caused the collapse.

She prayed she was wrong.

———

SEVERAL TENSE HOURS LATER, CLAIRE'S GREATEST FEAR WAS confirmed. She stood beside her parents in the hospital corridor while a grim-faced DI Ramsbottom relayed the news.

"The toxicology screening shows high levels of foxglove poison in her system," he stated. "Just like Nigella, except the levels are much higher. Whoever poisoned her intended to kill her. It's nearly miraculous she's still alive."

"Nigella didn't have the opportunity to get to a hospital in time," Alan reminded him, running a hand over the light stubble on his jaw. "Sarah was lucky not to be alone."

"I… I almost cancelled the interview," Janet said, staring blankly at the wall. "What if she'd been at home with her kids… What if…"

"Best not to play that game, dear," Alan said.

Claire sighed, wrapping her arms around herself. "Whoever did this is still out there."

Ramsbottom nodded. "And growing bolder. Poisoning

a second victim so soon after the first takes a lot of nerve."

"The poor girl," Janet murmured, dabbing at her eyes with a tissue. "The way I spoke to her earlier this week… She's just a young mum trying to make ends meet. Someone will need to look after her children, Harry."

"She has an aunt who lives a few floors down in Lowry Tower. They're being taken care of, I assure you," Ramsbottom said. He dug in his pocket and produced a notepad; a pink prawn cocktail crisp packet fell out with it. "I do have some positive news to share. Your hunch was spot-on, Claire. Forensics found traces of foxglove in the residue on the café floor. So, she was poisoned via her tea. I suppose that narrows things down to whoever had access to her cup at the garden centre."

Although Claire appreciated the validation, it was little comfort with a killer still on the loose. She met the inspector's gaze. "What happens now?"

Ramsbottom flipped to another page. "I suppose we figure out whom Sarah had contact with before she visited the cul-de-sac. I'll start by asking around the—"

"Bernard," Claire cut in, her eyes homing in on the same wall her mother had been staring at. "When I was at Meadowview this morning, Sarah was there to try to get her old job back. He had a tray with two cups of tea."

"Are you sure?"

"Certain," Claire said, swallowing down any doubt. "I

threw his business card onto the tray. I didn't see where he'd carried them from, but he carried them into the office where Sarah was waiting. I didn't see her drink it, but—"

"That's more than enough to have him brought in for questioning," Ramsbottom said, jotting down the detail. "Anything else?"

"Bernard purchased a large quantity of foxglove plants for the garden centre," Alan said. "I saw the invoices with my own eyes on his desk. I think you have a new prime suspect, Harry."

"And aren't I glad for it," Ramsbottom said, tucking the pad away. "Because I really thought it was Sarah. We've had witnesses claim that Nigella and Sarah might have been having some sort of love affair, and I was starting to wonder if Sarah killed Nigella over a lover's tiff. I'll put out a call for Bernard's immediate arrest."

Before they exited the hospital into the grey evening, Claire checked on Sarah again. She was still unconscious in the hospital bed, with machines breathing for her. It had been an exhausting and emotional day. But Sarah's plight had only strengthened Claire's resolve to uncover the truth behind the venomous deeds in Northash.

The murderer had proven their sting.

Claire had to stop a third cup of tea from succumbing to a foxglove infusion.

CLAIRE DRAGGED HER FEET ACROSS THE CUL-DE-SAC AS SHE set off from her parents' house after another shed talk with her father. Emotionally and physically drained after the day's traumatic events, she noticed Sally's car still parked outside Mrs Beaton's house and wandered over.

"No luck selling?" Claire asked, noting Sally's deflated expression.

"Not one bite. I've been advertising this open day for weeks, but the place is just too dated and run-down for most buyers. Everyone wants move-in ready these days, not a full renovation."

"Would feel strange to see that place looking any different," Claire mused, glancing back at the dark windows of the empty house—rundown for as long as her memories stretched back, and the only one in the cul-de-sac not living up to middle-class perfection. "Heading back to town?"

"Hop in," Sally said, reaching across to the passenger seat. "How about a nightcap at yours? After a day of pretending that place isn't a total dump, I think the only cure is a glass of red wine and a Claire catch-up."

Despite her exhaustion, Claire didn't have the heart to turn down her friend. Besides, a frivolous conversation with Sally over a glass of wine did sound like what she needed. "Sounds like a plan. We'll need to stop off somewhere because I don't have a drop in the—"

Claire's feet clanked against glass bottles in a plastic bag in the footwell.

"I knew it was going to be one of those days when I went shopping this morning," Sally said, a hint of defensiveness accompanied by a cheeky smile on her face. "And the kids are with their dad until Monday."

They drove down to Claire's flat, both ready to unwind after their separate emotional roller coasters. After pouring two glasses and curling up with the cats on the sofa, a black cherry candle burning on the coffee table, Claire filled Sally in on what had happened. She discussed the conversation she'd had with Tom and Hayley by the hives that morning, Bernard's callous business practices and his sketchy invoices and emails, Fiona's rush to sell her house and leave the country, and worst of all, Sarah's poisoning.

"And suddenly my problems feel tiny," Sally murmured, deep into her first glass. "I can't believe Northash has a proper poisoner running about. I know we've had our share of barmy murder cases these past few years, but this is like something out of 'Midsomer Murders.'"

Claire sighed. "I know. And they came so close to claiming a second victim."

"But at least the police are finally taking real action,"

Sally pointed out, topping up their glasses before they had a chance to drain them. "One, you might be able to write off as an accident, but two? From the sounds of it, Bernard's the man they're looking for."

"I hope so. Regardless of what she did or didn't do, Sarah didn't deserve any of this."

"Two kids," Sally shook her head, clutching her glass close to her chest. "Talk about the right place, right time tonight. If I were going to pass out in anyone's house, I'd want it to be Janet and Alan's." A thoughtful look crossed Sally's face. "Speaking of your parents, how are things going with your dad and that new job? I was surprised to see him in a uniform again after his..." She gestured down to her foot.

Despite everything, Claire smiled. "Before all of this started, I think he was in his element. Though, saying that, as much as he enjoys gardening, I know he misses the puzzle-solving element of police work. He was sticking notes all over the walls of his shed when I left him earlier."

"DI Harris back on the scene with his trusty sidekick?" Sally winked at her. "Or is he your sidekick?"

Claire considered her answer. "I'm not sure. After tonight, we might be off the case, anyway. Ramsbottom might be extracting a confession from Bernard as we speak."

"Unlikely." Sally arched an eyebrow. "Some kids

kicked a ball through my next-door neighbour's window last week, and he tried to suggest a gust of wind carried it when the kids swore blind they were playing football in the park. Something tells me the Harris partners-in-crime will get there first."

Claire laughed. "I suppose we do make a pretty good team."

The warmth of the wine was making her pleasantly relaxed, and the mention of 'team' sent her mind straight to relationships. Once upon a time, Claire had been the eternally single friend, and Sally had been in an apparently perfect marriage; but how times had changed.

"How are things going with you and Damon these days?"

A slow, happy smile spread across Sally's face. "Really, *really* good. Sometimes I wonder if we're still in the honeymoon phase. I keep waiting for the other shoe to drop. I mean, look at this idiot." She produced her phone and showed Claire a selfie Damon had sent. He was leaning forward in his gaming chair, headset primed, eyes on the screen, and the caption read, 'Wish me luck as I venture into battle.' "On paper, we have nothing in common, but I honestly can't remember the last time I felt this way about anyone. How did I fall in love with Northash's biggest nerd?"

"Because Northash's biggest nerd is also its biggest teddy bear. I'm so happy for you both."

"Honestly, Claire, all those years working next to him at the factory, how didn't you fall in love with him?" Sally laughed, draining her glass. "I used to swear he fancied you rotten. Surprised he never made a move."

Claire smiled to herself; she'd only ever been in love with one man.

"I know that smile," Sally said, nudging her arm. "How are things with you and Ryan?"

"Good, I think," Claire answered honestly. "He's been working a lot more lately, and he seems…" She swirled her glass, searching for the right words as Domino stretched out between them before sauntering off to the bedroom. "Unsettled? He thinks he's not giving the kids enough. Was talking about moving somewhere with cheaper house prices. I think he's nostalgic for his childhood—big house, big garden, all that. And I… I'm worried…"

"You're worried you're going to lose him again?" Sally filled in the blank before the air had a chance to settle. "He's crazy about you, Claire. He's a single dad in his mid-thirties. Professionally speaking, I think he's at least fifteen years too late for the big house and big garden on what he's earning at the gym. Have you thought about… you know… moving in together?"

Claire reached for the wine this time and topped up their glasses.

"I have," Claire said, "but with all his talk of wanting

to move somewhere bigger for the kids, he hasn't mentioned me in the equation, so I'm not sure."

Sally arched an eyebrow.

"You forget, I know you, Claire. You might have more of a grasp on your life these days, but when it comes to matters of the heart, you're as avoidant as they come. Remember when you weren't sure if he loved you because he hadn't told you, and you got yourself all worked up about not wanting to tell him that you loved him?"

Sighing, Claire nodded. She did have a habit of keeping things bottled up when it came to Ryan, but she'd had too many years of practice. Back when they were all teens, only Sally had known about her secret affections for her neighbour.

"Listen," Sally said, pausing to sip her wine. Her words were starting to slur a little. "In my professional opinion, it makes financial sense to combine incomes if you're serious about being together long term. Unless those are your Nintendo cartridges and colouring pencils on the dining table, it seems like you're halfway to living together as it is."

"But Ryan hasn't—"

"Ryan is the shyest man I've ever met," Sally interrupted, rolling her eyes. "I work with a guy who's exactly like him. Grew up chubby, now has an eight-pack, and yet he still can't lift his eyes off the ground whenever

Nancy walks in. He fancies her rotten, and everyone knows it. She knows it too, but that little insecure kid is still running the show. I tried my best to bite back when idiots dared to bully you back in school, but Ryan hung out with the art kids, and you know how they were treated. Abs or not, Ryan is still that sensitive, chubby kid hiding out in the art block." She drank more wine, and she wasn't done. "And like I said, it makes sense to combine your incomes. You must make decent money in the shop, and Ryan's gym salary would stretch further if his domestic outgoings were halved. You'd be surprised at the kind of mortgage you could get together."

"We're not even married."

"*So?*" Sally rolled her eyes. "A mortgage is basically marriage for us millennials. Take Mrs Beaton's old place, for example. It's almost identical in layout to the house next to your mum and dad's, but it's a third cheaper. A lick of paint and some new fixtures and fittings, and it would be worth the same. That big back garden would be ideal for the kids."

The idea was tempting—perhaps that was the wine talking—but it still felt like a pipe dream.

"Ryan would have to be on board, and—"

"*Just* an idea," Sally said breezily, her eyelids fluttering as she waved her glass around. "Or he just moves in here. You own this place since Em gifted you the building from her inheritance, so you could save up a deposit just like *that.*" She snapped her fingers, sloshing wine onto the sofa. "*Whoops*! Can you tell it's been a while? Gone right to my head."

Claire yawned. "Mine too."

"Can I have the sofa tonight? Not sure I fancy venturing out this late."

"All yours."

With Sally's 'professional' opinions swirling around, mingled with the red wine, Claire took a bathroom break before grabbing a duvet for Sally from the spare room. She wasted no time getting cosy, looking as on the verge of sleep as Claire felt.

"I almost forgot some juicy gossip I heard at work today," Sally said, stifling a yawn. "Fiona asked us to check over her house paperwork for when she'll need to send it to the solicitor if she gets an offer. I don't think she realised she'd included some of her bank statements along with her boiler certificate."

"Find anything good?"

"Fiona and Nigella had a joint account," Sally continued, settling on the sofa. "Given the payment reference Fiona was using, it looks like she's been siphoning money into a separate account since before Christmas."

"What was the payment reference?"

"*Escape.*" Sally closed her eyes and pulled the duvet tight. "Don't let me sleep in too long tomorrow. I promised Damon I'd join him for a comic book convention, which is a sentence I never thought I'd say."

Suddenly wide awake as she changed into her pyjamas in her bedroom, Claire thought back to the phone call she'd overheard between Fiona and an unknown person, to whom she'd said 'I love you.' A secret Portuguese lover? Any thoughts that Fiona's urgency to leave was driven by grief vanished. If she'd been moving money since before Christmas, and had only delivered the ultimatum to Nigella in February, there was more to this story than the widow had shared.

Claire didn't know if Fiona had been at the garden centre when Nigella was poisoned. But Fiona had been lingering by the seed packets, chatting to a mysterious person on the phone about her 'escape,' while the woman who'd kissed her wife multiple times ingested near-fatal foxglove poison just a stone's throw away.

Regardless of Bernard being in custody, Claire needed to speak to Fiona again.

CHAPTER TEN

*T*he sun shone down on Starfall Park, warm but not too hot for a lazy Sunday afternoon. Claire smiled as she watched Ryan chase Amelia and Hugo around the grassy field while their laughter filled the air. After their picnic of sandwiches and crisps, they ventured down to the duck pond, tossing their leftover crusts to the ducklings trailing behind their mothers.

Back at the flat, they baked—and burnt—chocolate-chip cookies, and played board games late into the evening. Seeing the children with their chocolatey smiles fighting over Monopoly, Claire couldn't deny that their lazy Sundays together had become her favourite day of the week.

On Monday morning, after replying to a message from Ryan that she'd pick the kids up from school later, her father walked in wearing his green polo uniform. Over cups of fresh coffee, Alan revealed that Sarah's condition was still critical but stable. The doctors said she wouldn't be well enough for questioning anytime soon.

"I'm going to pop into the garden centre today to have a chat with Bernard if he's out on bail," Alan said. "And I'll try speaking with Tom and Hayley too, to see if I can learn anything more about Nigella."

Claire nodded as her phone buzzed with an incoming text:

SALLY

Got you a second viewing with Fiona today at 1. I'll pick you up at the shop.

With Alan covering the garden-centre angle, she could focus her efforts on unravelling the mystery surrounding Fiona. Between the money siphoning and her eagerness to flee the country, Claire's instincts told her the widow was hiding something.

The hours raced along, bringing the warm spring morning to a close. As noon approached, the bright skies began to dim as clouds rolled in like a gloomy tide. Damon arrived for his late-Monday start, just in time for Claire to hop into Sally's car.

Her anticipation built as she and Sally drove past the large family homes on Wordsworth Avenue under a thick blanket of clouds. Dusting cat hair off her black blazer, Claire prepared herself to confront the widow again. As they walked up the pathway, Sally turned to her with a nervous smile.

"Ready?"

"As I'll ever be," Claire replied.

The door opened almost instantly after Sally's knuckles rapped on the polished wood.

"You again," Fiona said, no hint of the friendliness from their first meeting. "My brother warned me about you snooping around. You have no intention of putting in an offer for this house, do you?"

Claire felt a momentary temptation to retreat, but squared her shoulders instead. There went her plan to drop in subtle questions while pretending to take in the fixtures and fittings.

"Busted," Claire admitted, her tight smile going unreturned. "Your house is lovely, but no, I don't think any bank in their right mind would approve me for a mortgage for this place. I'm sorry for wasting your time, but—"

"You're right." Fiona's eyes turned to ice as she made a move to shut the door. "You are wasting my time. I think you should leave."

But Claire was quicker than Fiona's door slam. She wedged her foot into the doorframe, halting its movement. She bit back the pain, thankful Fiona didn't go for a second slam. Fiona left the door open, arching a brow at Claire, no doubt for her audacity.

"I only have a few questions," Claire said, moving her foot away. "If you have nothing to hide, then a conversation shouldn't be a problem, right?"

Fiona's features twisted in annoyance as she checked her watch. "Five minutes. And not a second more."

Claire wasted no time and decided to jump straight to the point. "I know you've been siphoning money from your joint account with Nigella, even before your separation. I also know about your plan to move to Portugal once you've sold this place, which you put up for sale the day after Nigella died. The timing doesn't look too good, does it?"

The widow chuckled, but it was far from warm. "You're clueless about the realities of marriage if you think any of that suggests I had a role in Nigella's death. Our marriage didn't end when I delivered my ultimatum; that's just when I gave up the fight. You wouldn't know that because you don't know anything about the life we had together."

Claire knew that Nigella had shared a New Year's kiss with a woman who was now fighting for her life after being poisoned, but she kept that to herself. She didn't know if Fiona knew about the moment, and if she didn't, Claire wasn't going to be the one to reveal a dead woman's secrets.

"So, fill me in," Claire said.

Fiona sighed, checking her watch again. "We met during a health-kick phase I was going through. Nigella was working behind the counter in a little health food shop over in Hebden Bridge. We started talking, and she told me all about her dream of starting a sustainable honey brand. I was charmed by her passion for her dream, and to be honest, I find ambition more attractive than anything." She scanned Claire's 'mortgage outfit,' with an arching brow, as though realising it had to be a costume. "My brother told me you run a little candle shop in the square, so you'll know dreams don't pay the bills."

"If only."

"Nigella didn't care about profit," Fiona continued, her gaze drifting past Claire to the houses across the road and beyond. "I should have seen the writing on the wall in the early days. She contributed nothing to that joint account. That money you claim I was 'siphoning' was money I put in. And Nigella had no qualms about withdrawing whatever she felt like when she needed something for the bees. I shouldered everything while she chased her fantasy. Nigella wasn't the only one with a dream." She glanced over her shoulder at the empty house. "The day I viewed this place, I imagined it would be filled with love and laughter. I thought we'd raise children here. But what did I get instead? An empty house and a life to restart on my own at nearly fifty."

"I'm sorry things didn't work out the way you wanted," Claire said. "What about the person on the phone? The one you said that you loved?"

Fiona laughed, a dry, cynical sound. "That's none of your business."

"And Portugal?"

"I was offered a headmaster job at a private school that significantly increases my salary," she said, her cold eyes narrowing on Claire. "I couldn't have accepted the position with Nigella dragging out the divorce the way she was. But the day after she died, they sent me a final email to confirm my interest, and I didn't hesitate to accept and put the house on the market. Nigella won't hold my future hostage any longer."

Claire's mind raced as she processed Fiona's revelations. She couldn't deny the sympathy tugging at her heart for the bitter widow. Fiona had clearly loved and supported Nigella in the early days of their relationship, only to end up feeling used and discarded in the end. Her anger was understandable, as was her eagerness to start fresh overseas now that she was finally free from the stagnant marriage.

Yet as much as Claire wanted to take Fiona at her word, doubts still lingered. The timing of putting the house up for sale and accepting the new job was awfully convenient. And Fiona had avoided revealing who her mysterious overseas phone contact was. Claire yearned to believe the best in people, but her instincts wouldn't allow her to cross Fiona off the suspect list just yet. There were still too many unanswered questions surrounding her hasty actions after Nigella's untimely demise.

Sighing, Claire knew she had one card left to play.

"Did you hear about the second poisoning?"

"Of my Lowry Tower waitress replacement, you mean?" Fiona said bitterly. "Seems like Nigella was getting the low-stakes, low-cost life she clearly craved. Now, I'd say that your time is up, Claire." Fiona's eyes blazed as she turned to Sally. "And don't think you'll be getting away with this. Your facilitation of this intrusion is grossly unprofessional. I'll make sure your manager knows why I'm switching estate agents."

The door slammed with a heavy, echoing thud, as if to punctuate Fiona's last words. Claire felt a droplet of water on her forehead, and she looked up to the grey clouds obscuring the sun. The bitter aftertaste of Fiona's final comment about her 'Lowry Tower waitress replacement' reverberated as the rain started.

"Sally, I'm really sorry if I've jeopardised your job," Claire said as they set off to the car. "I'll never forgive myself if you get fired over this."

Before Sally could respond, the growl of an engine sliced through the air, and a beat-up Land Rover skidded to a stop beside them. The door flung open, and Tom stepped out, his face as annoyed as Fiona's when she'd first answered the door. Hands buried deep in his pockets, he approached them with a stare like smouldering coals.

"What are you doing here again, Claire?" Before Claire could formulate a reply, Tom spoke, "Why don't you stick to your candles? My sister and I have gone through enough without you sticking your nose into our lives."

Sally looked at Claire, her eyes widening ever so slightly—a silent suggestion that perhaps it was time to leave. Yet something in Claire—whether it be her father's determination or her mother's stubbornness—refused to back down.

"How did you end up becoming Nigella's business partner, Tom?"

Tom looked at the house as the raindrops thickened, but he lingered by the closed gate, pushing his hands deeper into his pockets.

"I used to be a financial adviser for a city bank," he said, nodding off in some obscure direction that Claire thought might be Manchester. "I looked at Nigella's failing honey operation as a favour to my sister and agreed to invest to help grow things. I saw potential and tried to help turn it around, but let's face it, when it came to making money, Nigella was a lost cause."

Tom's height allowed him to step over the gate with ease, bypassing it altogether. The front door slammed again, echoing down the street as Claire slid into the car beside Sally. Rain hammered against the windshield in relentless torrents, amplifying the thick atmosphere that filled the air between the two old friends.

"Sally, I'm really sorry if—"

"Don't worry about it, Claire," Sally said, although worry tinged her tone. "The viewing was my idea, remember? I'm a top seller at Smith and Smith. I'm sure I'll be fine."

Claire's chest knotted with concern at the sound of one of her oldest friends trying to reassure herself. She hoped Sally wouldn't face any repercussions for her involvement in the ill-fated visit.

Claire had hoped to clarify the situation with Fiona, but she'd only painted herself in a guiltier shade—not just for her estranged wife, but for the 'Lowry Tower waitress replacement' as well.

As they drove away, a conversation she'd had with Nigella about 'replacements' wriggled free from her memories, and more specifically, the explanation of the queen bee being replaced with a younger model.

Is that what Nigella had tried to do?

Replace Fiona with Sarah?

THE RAIN POURED DOWN IN UNRELENTING SHEETS OVER Meadowview Garden Centre as Claire dashed from Sally's car, her head barely shielded by the jacket pulled up over it. Taking a fortifying breath, Claire hurried inside and scanned for her father's familiar frame among the greenery.

She found him pruning back the dead heads on a table of potted roses, snipping with practised motions. Claire waited until he set down the blades before updating him on the confrontational visit with Fiona.

He listened intently as Claire recounted Fiona's odd behaviours—the overseas job offer accepted so soon after Nigella's death, the mysterious phone contact she was supposedly in love with, her rush to sell their marital home, and her comment about Nigella's 'replacement' being lined up.

"It does seem suspicious, little one," Alan admitted, dusting potting soil from his hands. "Almost like she was waiting for Nigella to be out of the picture before she made her big move. I've been thinking about the method a lot this afternoon."

"The poison?"

"It's a rather vicious method, don't you think?" he mused in a low voice. "Like the murderer wanted Nigella —and Sarah—to suffer. Now that we know Fiona knew about Sarah... just something to consider."

"She was here when Sarah was poisoned," Claire said,

craning her neck to look at the seed-packet racks. "I should have asked about her alibi for Nigella's death."

"Perhaps, but you gained some valuable information. I did ask Harry about her alibi this morning, and he…" Her father paused to sigh as his eyes met Claire's. "He politely suggested we stay out of the investigation from now on. I think he believes he's gained all the information he will from us."

"Does that mean he's close to cracking the case?"

"Given how stressed he sounded on the phone, I doubt it. He had to release Bernard for lack of evidence. It turns out the invoice and emails I found weren't enough to convict him, and he claims there was a period of at least five minutes when he left the teabags to steep unattended in the café's kitchen." He cast a glance in the direction of the café. "I've been hoping to speak with him all morning, but he's yet to leave his office. Tom was here earlier, but I couldn't get him to stand still long enough to chat."

"He turned up as I was leaving Fiona's," she revealed. "He said he acted as Nigella's financial adviser to help the struggling business. Made out like it was a favour to Fiona."

"They did seem friendly when they were at the cul-de-sac for whisky, but I suppose that makes sense knowing they were in-laws." Alan brushed the cuttings into a bin and dusted off his hands. "Makes you wonder why he isn't more interested in justice, and I could say the same for Fiona. We'll have to keep an eye on the siblings. See if we can figure out where their true allegiances lie."

"Not heeding Harry Ramsbottom's warning, then?"

He winked as he patted Claire's cheek. "What do you think, little one? Now, I should get back to pruning. The delphiniums are on the verge of mutiny. But you go on and see if you can chat with Hayley. Last I saw, she was in the beekeeping nook. Might have something useful to share about her mentor without Tom casting a shadow over her."

Claire ventured to the back of the garden centre, where she found Hayley tucked away from the rain inside the small beekeeping shed with an unlikely visitor.

"Ah, Claire!" Em beamed, ushering her inside. "Just the woman we were talking about. Fancy giving us a hand?"

Hayley was busy jarring up honey from a vat, the golden liquid pouring in a smooth arc into the glass jar she held below the spout. Em stood beside her, passing her empty jars with both hands, like a well-rehearsed assembly line. Claire noticed a stack of 'Nigella's Honey' stickers on a nearby table and got to work copying the positioning from the finished jars lining the shelves. The two wildflower candles Claire had given to Nigella stood out, and she'd never know if Nigella ever got around to smelling them.

Claire comfortably slipped into her old factory role of sticker-applier on the assembly line while Em explained that Hayley was a frequent attender of Em's yoga classes. Em had dropped by to see how the young apprentice was holding up after seeming rather distracted during that morning's class. Em claimed she was there to buy wildflowers to liven up her houseboat too, but Claire wouldn't put it past Em to go out of her way to check on someone she knew was struggling.

"Hayley was just telling me something rather interesting about our poor poisoned beekeeper," Em said, her wispy voice lowered as she retrieved a fresh box of glass jars. "I suggested she should share the information with you, and fate sent you through the door."

Fate, and Claire's hunger for the truth.

"I'm all ears," Claire said, pressing another sticker onto a jar and sliding it aside.

Hayley hesitated as she dunked the ladle into the vat. "Oh, I don't know. It's probably nothing."

Claire leaned forward, intrigued. "Please, anything at all might help."

"Well..." Hayley set down her ladle with a sigh. "A few weeks back, before I heard about the stolen equipment turning up for sale online, I saw someone packing up half the contents of this shed into duffel bags early one morning. At the time, I assumed it was Nigella having a clear-out, but now…"

"Now you think you saw the thief," Claire finished.

Hayley nodded. "I know I should've said something sooner, but I didn't think anything of it until the police questioned me about my alibi." She dunked the ladle into the vat of runny honey, and her eyes met Claire's. She must have picked up on the expectation in Claire's eyes because she explained, "I was helping my grandmother bake for the church fete with her choir friends. The police have already confirmed it."

Claire filed the information aside, more interested in what she'd seen that early morning. "Can you remember anything about what this person looked like? Any little detail might help identify who it was."

Hayley's nose scrunched up in concentration. "That's the thing. I have no idea. Whoever it was had on a full beekeeper's outfit—gloves, netted hat, the full suit. That's why I thought it was Nigella, but she rarely wore the gear. She used to say that the gloves and netting got in the way of her 'sensory experience' with the bees. She liked the tactile feedback, claimed it helped her get a better grip on the frames and manage the hive more effectively."

"But wouldn't she worry about stings?" Em asked.

"Nigella had been with that colony for years," Hayley said, casting a sad glance at the hives. "She had bred them to be rather gentle and knew their behaviour like the back of her hand. She was nothing short of an expert. She knew exactly when she could approach them and when it was better to keep her distance, just from a glance. I learned so much from her in my short time here, but I don't think I'll ever be able to read them like Nigella did."

"So, Nigella would never have gone through all that trouble of wearing a full beekeeper's outfit to pack some bags," Claire confirmed, ripping off a label that had gone on wonky. "This might be a stretch, but was the person quite tall?"

"I'm not sure. They were crouched over, and... Why did you ask if they were tall?" Her brows knitted together. "Are you suggesting it might have been Tom?"

"It might be nothing, but I saw him in a suit here," Claire said.

"Tom is scared of the bees, that's all," Hayley said, shaking her head. "He hasn't built up a tolerance to the venom from their stings like Nigella, but he wouldn't be the one stealing from the business. He's been trying his hardest to make it work, and he's been great with me since I started working under Nigella. She wasn't my only mentor. Tom's been teaching me all about the financial side of things. I appreciated Nigella's ethics and passion, but Tom is right. Without profit, we won't be able to pay the rent, and then what happens to the bees? Nigella could never look ahead; she was just laser-focused on caring for the colony. Tom wasn't the thief... but Nigella was adamant it was Sarah."

"And do you think it could be Sarah?"

Hayley didn't answer as she dripped the honey into a fresh jar.

"You know about their relationship," Claire stated.

"I wouldn't call it a *relationship*," Hayley said, staring ahead with a blank stare as she used the contraption that sealed on the airtight lid. "Nigella wasn't one to talk about her private life all that much, but I saw how Sarah acted around her. She was like a lovesick puppy. She'd show up with gifts and make grand declarations of love, but Nigella was adamant she wasn't interested."

"Sarah gave me the impression Nigella was rather taken with her," Claire countered.

"Nigella made it *clear* she had no intentions there," Hayley said firmly. "She knew there was too much of an age gap, without all the baggage, but I don't think she could get that through to Sarah. It started off as one drunken kiss on New Year's Eve. I think Nigella and Fiona had an argument at the party, and Fiona left early. As harsh as this sounds..." She paused, as though wondering if she should go further. "Nigella had no interest in being any sort of mother figure to anyone, let alone someone else's young kids. I even had to twist her arm to mentor me. She valued having a simple life. Nigella's parents were hardly around, and she had to bear the brunt of raising her siblings. I think she felt like she'd already ticked that box."

"That's understandable," Em said with a sad smile. "Sounds like someone who was selective about where she put her energy. A woman after my own heart. May she rest in peace now that the burden of life no longer troubles her."

"Do you know anything about Nigella's marriage?" Claire asked.

"They'd already separated by the time I started working under her," Hayley admitted, sliding another jar to Claire. "I was around when Fiona would show up with Tom sometimes. It always seemed like Fiona was poking for arguments, and Nigella would never rise to it. Fiona ended things over an ultimatum."

"Fiona or the bees," Claire repeated.

"Ultimatums never end well," Em stated. "It's a shortcut to resentment and mistrust."

"Which is why Nigella refused to choose."

"She didn't choose the bees?" Claire asked, the surprise clear in her voice.

"That's how Fiona perceived it, but what did she expect Nigella to do? Get rid of a large part of her life just because Fiona said so?" Hayley sighed, scraping up the last dregs of honey at the bottom of the vat. "Nigella was the one at home cooking dinner every night. She kept the house immaculate. Yet, from how Fiona acted, you'd think Nigella was some money-hungry vampire. That's not how I saw her. She simply didn't care enough about it to revolve her life around it."

"Truly a woman after my own heart," Em said, raising an empty glass to the sky.

"Nigella would've been content to live off the small amount of money she made from the honey," Hayley said, looking at the finished jars with a sad smile. "But Fiona's ambitions were set higher; no matter what Nigella earned, it was never good enough."

Piecing together Hayley's account with the snippets Fiona had shared on the doorstep about Nigella's reluctance to start a family, Claire started to see the bigger picture more clearly. Fiona and Nigella may have been incompatible from the get-go, even if they didn't recognise it when they met during Fiona's 'health-kick phase.'

"So Nigella wasn't delaying the divorce to take Fiona's money?"

"That's not how it seemed to me," Hayley admitted in a whisper. "To me, it seemed like Nigella was holding out in hopes they'd reconcile. I didn't get it. It was as if Nigella was in love with some version of Fiona I never met."

Claire wondered how different the 'health-kick' Fiona could be from her current polished and professional iteration. Perhaps she'd also been in a 'I don't want children' phase to match.

"Then why would Fiona claim that Nigella wanted all her money?" Claire wondered aloud.

"Perhaps to a greedy person, that's how it felt," Em said, sliding the final jar from the box to Hayley to fill with the last of the honey. "Classic projection, and it's not as if Nigella can defend herself anymore. It's good she still has people looking after her memory. I have to get to the gym for my half-past-three yoga class, but I hope you're feeling better now that you've got some things off your chest."

"Yes, I am, actually," Hayley said, her face brightening with a smile. "Thank you, Em. And please, take a jar for yourself. You too, Claire."

"Vegan," Em said with a wink, "but the offer was a kind one."

Claire wanted to refuse as well, given the jars that had been left on her doorstep and her father's potting desk, but Hayley looked at her expectantly, so Claire accepted with a grateful smile.

"Not as thick as it used to be," Hayley said with a sigh. "It's almost as if the bees are stressed and know Nigella isn't around anymore."

"Then it's a good thing they have you to look after them," Em assured her, hugging her. "Claire, if you're ready, shall we walk back to the village together?"

They left Hayley to her tasks and set off into the rain towards the garden centre. When they were out of earshot of the hives, Claire turned to Em and asked, "How well do you know Hayley? Do you trust her?"

Em nodded firmly. "Hayley is a sweet and honest girl. She's been attending my yoga classes since she was a teenager. I believe what she told us."

Claire nodded. She trusted Em's judgment, so she chose to trust Hayley's account, even though it contradicted much of what Fiona had claimed earlier. With Fiona planning to leave the country, Claire suspected she was the less reliable narrator.

Just as they stepped into the covered area, Alan hurried over in his coat. "Claire, I have some news. Sarah is awake and talking!"

A sigh of relief escaped Claire. "When can we see her?"

"Right now. She's specifically asked for *us*."

Claire's pulse quickened with anticipation; this could be the break in the case they needed. They headed for the car as the rain continued to fall. Alan offered Em a lift into the village, but she declined. "Feeling the rain on your skin is a privilege," she said mysteriously before walking away.

Claire was glad to have a friend like Em to keep her grounded, though she wished Em were joining them for support. Given what Sarah had endured these past few days, Claire wasn't sure what awaited them at the hospital.

"She asked to speak with us?" Claire echoed as Meadowview shrank in the rear-view mirror.

He turned down Radio Four with a solemn nod. "Apparently, she has some confessions to make."

CHAPTER ELEVEN

*T*he comforting aroma of chicken soup filled the air, wafting along with a passing lunch trolley as Claire and her father made their way down the hospital's austere corridor. Ahead, DI Ramsbottom punched buttons on a vending machine while attacking a pasty, sprinkling crumbs over the gleaming linoleum. Alan cleared his throat, diverting Ramsbottom's attention from the lacklustre hot chocolate dribbling into a flimsy cardboard cup.

"Ah, there you are!" Ramsbottom exclaimed. "I was starting to think you'd stood me up."

"I was waiting for Claire," Alan replied, engaging in a firm handshake with his old colleague. "Mind you, after your warning to keep our noses out, I wasn't sure we'd be welcome."

"No hard feelings, old chap. You know how it is. Civilians and poisoning cases don't mix well, do they? Safety first." Ramsbottom yanked the cup from the machine and cautiously sniffed the greyish, steaming liquid. "But every cloud has a silver lining, eh? Sarah's recovery has saved us the disgrace of having *two* unsolved poisonings in a single week."

"Just one fatal poisoning and a near-fatal poisoning," Alan said with a thoughtful nod, his sarcasm going unnoticed. "Is Sarah on the ward?"

"She's in her own room and refusing to talk to us. Whatever she wants to confess, she wants you two to hear it before we do." He sighed before taking another bite of his pasty. "I tried to pressure it out of her, but you know how defensive the nurses get. I expect you to tell me everything she shares with you."

Leaving Ramsbottom to his dodgy hot chocolate, Claire and Alan continued walking. Claire was curious— what could Sarah possibly want to tell them? Was she worried about being arrested for what she knew? The word 'confession' had been bugging her since they left Meadowview.

The sterile scent of antiseptic hung heavy in the air of Sarah's dimly lit room, silent except for the beeping machines. Propped up in bed, crisp white sheets washed out her face, her complexion as grey as the vending machine hot chocolate. An older woman, probably the aunt who lived in the same building, dabbed at the corners of her eyes while Sarah's two children showed off their homemade 'Get Well Soon Mummy' cards. Sarah's eyes teared up as she looked at the cards, wincing as she moved to prop them up on the bedside table. After an awkward moment of Claire and her father lingering at the back of the room, the aunt took the kids to the café downstairs to give 'Mummy and her friends' some privacy.

"How are you holding up?" Claire asked, sliding into a chair beside the bed.

"Feels like the world's worst hangover," Sarah rasped, eyeing a cup of water. Claire passed it over, and Sarah sank back into her crinkly pillows. "They say I've been out for days, but it feels like I could still sleep forever."

"You'll come around in time. Your body has been fighting something most people wouldn't survive," Alan said, leaning on his cane at the foot of the bed. "Do you have any idea who did this to you?"

Sarah's face clouded as if sifting through a fog of memories. After a thoughtful pause, she shook her head, her eyes beginning to glisten. Claire grabbed a tissue from a nearby box and handed it to Sarah, who offered a shaky but appreciative smile.

"I'm sorry," Sarah said, her voice barely above a whisper. "I'm still trying to make sense of that day. All I remember is heading to the garden centre and then to the cul-de-sac for the interview. Everything else is fuzzy."

"That's understandable, given what you've been through," Alan replied. "So, you were looking to get your old job back from Bernard after quitting?"

"Seemed easier than braving a call to Janet," Sarah said, emitting a shaky laugh. "Bernard offered to take me back, but at minimum wage and with fewer hours. He knows I've been scraping by for months. I kept asking for more shifts, but he always brushed me off."

Claire sighed, baffled by the man's audacity. "Notice anything odd about your tea?"

"Don't think so."

Alan stepped closer to her bed, curiosity in his eyes. "You mentioned confessions? There's no time like the present."

Dropping her shoulders, she whispered, "I'm so ashamed. Desperation got the better of me. I've got mouths to feed and bills piling up, and—"

Her voice faltered, breaking into ragged sobs. Claire handed her another tissue.

"You're the thief," Alan surmised. His voice was gentle, devoid of judgment.

"I *only* stole the coffee beans, I swear!" Sarah tried to sit up, grimacing as pain forced her back down. "And Janet was right. I did take her purse. This isn't *me*, not normally."

"Explain," Alan urged, tranquil as a still lake.

"It was a moment of madness. I spotted the cash spilling out of her purse in her handbag. She was distracted on the phone, and something took over me, and before I knew it, the purse was in my hand." Her eyes, red-rimmed, seemed to lose their light, and her mouth sagged. "I was going to return it, but then Janet realised it was gone. She raised the alarm, and I panicked. I should've come clean. But when the police arrived, I figured they'd pin the other thefts on me. So, I hid the purse somewhere I knew they would find it and waited to see how things would unfold."

Sarah's eyes darted between Claire and her father, gauging their reactions. Claire, however, along with Alan, had already suspected as much. For all her theatricality, Janet wouldn't have made such an accusation without being sure.

"You didn't, by any chance, don a beekeeper's suit to loot Nigella's shed, did you?" Claire couldn't help but ask.

"Or sneak into the stockroom for a quick tool heist?" Alan added.

"I *swear* on my life, I didn't steal anything else. I'd never have pocketed those coffee beans if someone else hadn't already been thieving. Stupidly, I thought I could get away with it too. What an idiot I've been."

Alan's lips curved into a tight smile. "We all have our foolish moments, my dear. You showed guts in coming clean. Better late than never. Any inkling who the other thief might be?"

Sarah shook her head without needing to think about it. "Nigella only thought it was me when Bernard noticed bags of beans were going missing from the café. I denied it, but she could see right through me. Knowing I was lying about that made her think it was all me. She died thinking I'd do that to her." Her gaze dropped to the white sheets as her lashes batted out fresh tears. "I also lied about Nigella pursuing me."

"I know," Claire offered, wanting to spare her further embarrassment. "Nigella confided in Hayley about what happened after that first kiss."

"I don't know what came over me," she whispered. "That wasn't *me* either, but I developed these strong feelings for her. I felt so safe and warm in her presence. I just wanted to feel like that all the time. Nigella tried to let me down gently, but I couldn't stop myself."

Claire felt a twinge of sympathy, seeing the heartbreak in Sarah's eyes. "Do you know anything about Nigella's marriage to Fiona?"

"She refused to discuss it with me, even before the kiss," Sarah said, sniffing back the ebbing tears. "Nigella would come into the café every afternoon for a cup of tea at the same time, and she'd always make sure to ask how things were looking after the kids. She said she understood how tough it could be doing it alone. I'd always have her tea steeping in the back before she turned up."

"And she stuck to that routine till the end?" Alan asked.

"Every day," Sarah confirmed. "Even after rejecting all my advances. She wanted things to return to how they were before New Year's. She didn't seem to like change all that much."

"And the day she died," Alan said, pacing by the side of the bed with slow, measured steps. "You made her tea at…?"

"I always put the tea bag in around two-fifteen, and she'd always collect it around half past."

"So, in those fifteen minutes, the tea could have been tampered with?"

Sarah's brow furrowed as she struggled to recall the hazy details. Then, as if from nowhere, tears spilled down her cheeks. "Yes, that *is* what happened."

"How can you know that?" Claire asked, leaning forward.

"I… I don't know." She squinted ahead while her foggy mind dug for details. "I remembered something before everything went black. But I can't remember *what* I remembered." Her eyelids twitched as she clenched them tight. "There were *two* teabags in the cup. I flattened them against the side of the cup and then lifted them out with a spoon, and one of them fell on the floor.

I picked it up, and…" She let go of the tissue and turned over her right hand to show a dappled red rash stretching across her palm and fingers. "It gave me these marks."

"Foxglove is poisonous to the touch," Claire remembered aloud, picturing her father ripping up the plants while wearing gardening gloves. "Dad, you thought the foxglove was dried and turned to powder. It must have been sealed in a tea bag."

"It's seeming that way," he said, moving closer to Sarah. "But there's something else, isn't there? The rash is reminding you of something else."

Sarah moved the splotchy red marks closer to her face. "I… I can't remember."

"But there *is* something. *Think*, Sarah. Did you see someone else with a rash like that? Did you confront them?"

"I… I *can't* remember."

Just as Alan looked like he was going to push further, the door creaked open, and a nurse in pale-blue scrubs walked in. She moved over to the bed, her eyes flicking to the digital monitor displaying Sarah's vitals.

"Everything appears to be stable, Sarah," the nurse said, her professional tone softened by a kind smile. "We'll keep a close watch on you tonight. Visiting time is coming to an end. You need to rest."

"She's trying to remember something," Claire said. "Is

there any way to help jog her memory? It might help us figure out who poisoned her."

"Memory loss around traumatic events is not unheard of," the nurse offered with a thin smile that Claire knew meant 'there's nothing I can do.' "The memories could come back in their own time, or they might not. The brain has its own way of dealing with shock, and right now, rest is what Sarah needs more than anything."

Alan straightened up, his frustration giving way to a fatherly smile. "Thank you, Sarah. You've been a tremendous help. If you remember anything, anything at all, don't hesitate to get in touch."

"I will," Sarah rasped. "Nurse, could I please see my children again?"

"The best thing you can do for your children now is to get better. You'll be able to see them soon, I promise."

"Please," Sarah begged. "They're my world."

Sighing, the nurse promised to see what she could do before Claire and her father followed her into the corridor. Ramsbottom was shaking a bag of crisps by the vending machine, waving for Alan when their eyes met. Alan hobbled along to fill the DI in, and from the opposite direction, Sarah's two young children bounded towards the door, chased by their aunt.

"You'd think they were in a playground!" she exclaimed to Claire, shaking her head. "You got any?"

"Oh, I…"

Before Claire could consider her answer, her heart plummeted as if she'd been dragged over the steepest peak of a roller coaster. She patted her jacket in a desperate search for her phone, then noticed the clock on the wall ahead of her.

3:30 p.m.

She pictured Amelia and Hugo waiting outside the school gates, wondering where Claire was, thinking she'd forgotten them. She hadn't forgotten them; she'd just failed to remember *to* remember.

CHAPTER TWELVE

laire arrived at the school forty minutes after pickup time, her heart racing as her father pulled up outside the empty playground. She jumped out and scanned the area, dread rising in her chest—no sign of Amelia or Hugo waiting by the wall where she usually collected them.

Had they been allowed to walk home?

She rechecked her phone, but there were no messages from the school or Ryan.

She ran across the playground to the front doors and tugged at the heavy blue doors, but they didn't budge—locked. Peering through the narrow window, she saw the lights were still on inside.

"Hello?" she called through the glass, rapping her knuckles against the pane. "Is anyone there?"

A cleaner buffing the floor glanced up, and Claire waved wildly to get her attention. The woman shook her head, clearly unable to hear her through the door, and resumed polishing the tiles.

Claire groaned, dropping her forehead against the cold glass. She couldn't believe she'd lost track of time like this. After everything with Sarah, the thought of collecting the kids had completely slipped her mind.

She hammered on the door again until the cleaner looked back over with an irritated scowl. Claire pointed urgently to the door handle, pleading with her eyes for it to be opened. The woman held up a hand to signal her to wait and switched off the noisy buffing machine. Her rubber-soled shoes squeaked as she shuffled over, keys jangling in her hand.

"Thank you," Claire said as the door swung open. "I'm so sorry. I'm here to pick up Amelia and Hugo. Their father usually collects them, but I was supposed to do it today. I have a few times... I... Have they already gone home?"

The cleaner squinted at her over her glasses. "I'm just the cleaner, love. You'll have to ask inside."

Claire nodded and squeezed past the bulky cleaning trolley blocking the corridor. Her footsteps echoed down the empty hallway, dread swirling in the school she'd once attended. Rounding a corner, she spotted them sitting outside the reception office, alone but for a young female teacher standing by them. Relief washed over Claire at the sight of them.

"I'm so sorry," she said, rushing over. "I completely lost track of time."

"It's okay," Hugo mumbled, not glancing up from his video game.

Amelia fixed on her with a silent scowl.

"Are you their legal guardian?" the teacher asked. She looked barely older than a student herself, though she exuded maturity beyond her years.

"Oh, no, I'm their…" Claire stammered, thrown off guard. "I'm Claire. I really am so sorry about all this."

"She's not some weirdo, Miss," Amelia said. "She's telling the truth."

The teacher offered a polite smile. "We did try to call your husband, but there was no answer."

"He's at work, and we're not…" Claire stopped herself with an awkward laugh. "I'm his girlfriend."

"I see." The teacher nodded slowly, regarding her with an expression Claire couldn't quite decipher. "Well, since you're here now, do you mind if I have a quick word in private?"

Claire's chest constricted. She couldn't be in trouble, could she? It was an honest mistake, albeit an embarrassing one.

"Of course," she managed, signalling for the kids to

stay put while she followed the teacher into a small adjoining office.

"Take a seat." The teacher, Miss Marsden according to her dangling name badge, perched on the edge of the desk while Claire lowered herself onto a stiff chair, preparing for a reprimand. "I'm sure it was just an oversight, but we need you to ensure the children are picked up on time in the future."

Claire nodded, shamefaced. "I know, and I'm so sorry. It won't happen again."

"That said, I didn't want to talk to you about that." Marsden fidgeted with a pen on the desk. "I wanted to check in. See if everything is okay at home?"

"I'm not sure what you mean?"

"Well, we had a bit of an... incident today involving Amelia. I just wanted to ensure there weren't any issues we should be aware of?"

Claire's thoughts raced. Had something happened with one of the other kids? A spat or bullying? Amelia could be sensitive at times, loud and brash even, but she was a good kid.

"What sort of incident?" Claire asked carefully.

Miss Marsden inhaled deeply before responding. "Amelia was caught selling drawings to the other children at lunch. Apparently, she was proclaiming herself to be a 'future famous artist whose work would be worth a lot someday.' She encouraged the other children to 'invest early' while prices were still low."

"Kids, eh?" she said with an awkward laugh. "You know, back when I was at school, there was this one lad who'd try to sell cans of pop and chocolate bars from his backpack."

She remained straight-faced. "The concerning part was that Amelia claimed she was raising money for her father to buy them a new home."

Claire's laughter died. She recalled her hushed conversation with Ryan by the fence at the cul-de-sac, Amelia drawing under the tree nearby. Had she overheard them?

"I see," Claire said slowly. "Their dad wouldn't have put any pressure on her, if that's what you're worried about. He's currently under some work stress, and you know what kids are like." She imitated the sound of a sponge soaking up water. "You know?"

"I'm sure he didn't intentionally. But it's a big burden for a child to take on. Moving house can be very unsettling for young children."

"I'll talk to her, and her dad," Claire promised. "Smooth it all out. It won't happen again."

Miss Marsden finally cracked a real smile. "Amelia clearly has quite the little entrepreneurial streak and some real artistic talent. The drawings are very impressive for her age."

"I couldn't agree more," Claire said, standing up. "And again, I really am sorry for the lateness. It won't happen again."

"Make sure it doesn't," Miss Marsden said, offering Claire the door. "You know, Amelia talks about a 'Claire' sometimes. She speaks very highly of you. Seems like she's lucky to have a better step-mum than I did at her age."

Claire blinked in surprise, touched by the unexpected compliment. Before she could respond, the teacher bid her farewell and set off down the corridor in the opposite direction. Gathering the children, Claire repeated her apologies. Hugo mumbled that it was fine, and that their dad was late sometimes too, while Amelia trailed silently behind with a face like thunder. As they crossed the playground, Claire touched the girl's shoulder.

"Can I see the drawings you did today?"

Amelia unzipped her backpack with a dramatic puff and thrust a stack of pictures over without making eye contact. Claire flicked through the pages, marvelling at the skill on show in the pencil sketches of flowers—roses, tulips, hydrangeas. Then she stopped on one that made her blood run cold.

A meticulously shaded foxglove plant dominated the page, its poisonous, bell-shaped flowers and ruffled leaves captured in perfect detail. She thought back to

Amelia, hunched over her sketchpad under the tree while Claire talked to Ryan about his worries.

Claire crouched down to Amelia's level. "Listen, if you overheard your dad and me talking about grown-up problems, I want you to know that's not for you to fix, okay? Grown-ups worry about silly stuff sometimes."

Amelia scuffed her shoe on the ground. "I don't want to move to Burnley. I like our house, even without a treehouse."

Claire's chest tightened. She didn't want them to move away, either. "I know. I like your house too, and I'm sure your dad does. He wants what's best for you and Hugo, that's all." She hooked her finger under Amelia's down-turned chin and lifted it up. "So, how much did you rake in, future famous artist?"

"Twenty quid," Amelia said. "But I had to give it all back."

"Well, I hope you got your drawings back. That's just good business sense."

"I did."

"That's my girl." Claire pinched her cheek and handed back the drawings. Except for one. She pulled a crumpled twenty-pound note from her jacket pocket and stuffed it into Amelia's hand. "I'd like to buy this one of the foxgloves. Consider it an investment in your future art career."

Amelia eyed her suspiciously for a moment before holding the money up to the sunlight to check it was real.

"Nice doing business with you."

"Could you sign it for me?" Claire asked. "That way, when you're a famous artist one day, I can say I owned an early original."

The flattery worked, and Amelia fished a pencil from her bag and scrawled her name in the corner, leaning against Claire's leg as she did so.

"And stay away from these flowers if you ever see them growing anywhere, okay? Don't even touch them. Promise?"

Amelia nodded her promise before running off to join Hugo in the car. Claire looked down at the drawing; her art style was so much like how she remembered Ryan's being at that age. She hoped wherever Amelia's future took her, she'd follow her passion.

"No harm done, eh?" Alan said back in the car, looking down at the drawing. "This is smashing, Amelia. I hope you'll let me buy your next masterpiece."

"Thirty quid," Amelia said. "Get them while they're cheap."

Claire and her father both laughed, but his smile soured the longer he stared at the drawing.

"Can't stop thinking about that rash on Sarah's hand," he admitted in a whisper. "It's what triggered her memory of that extra teabag. What if… she saw matching marks on someone else?"

"The question is, who else has been handling foxglove?" Claire wondered as they drove away from the school. "And why haven't we noticed any rashes until today?"

ALAN DROPPED THEM OFF BY THE CLOCK TOWER, AND Claire shepherded Amelia and Hugo into The Hesketh Arms. Ryan would finish work in fifteen minutes, and Claire hoped he'd see her text message explaining what happened before he noticed the list of missed calls from the school.

With a group of young men crowding the pool table, Claire got them seated in a booth with their glasses of juice. Just as they settled, a large figure lumbered through the doorway. DI Ramsbottom made his way to the bar and ordered a meat pie before spotting Claire and waving her over.

"Afternoon, Claire. Fancy seeing you here," he said. "Your father filled me in on Sarah. Shame she still can't seem to remember whatever it is she's forgotten. I had my officers try again before the nurses kicked us out, but it's all a blank."

Claire bristled at his tone. "She's been through a lot,

Detective. I'm sure the memories will return when they're ready to."

"Well, we can't rule her out as a suspect until she does remember." His eyes lit up when the meat pie appeared in front of him. "She could still be lying, couldn't she? Admit to one lie, tell another. People can be rather devious, even on death's door."

Claire bit her tongue, refusing to rise to the bait. She changed the subject. "Did you confirm Hayley's alibi on the day Nigella was murdered? She said she was with her grandmother."

"Oh, right, yes. Checks out completely. Spent all morning baking, apparently. Several witnesses."

"And they're not covering for her?"

"Not unless her grandmother's baking buddies are all a bunch of liars?" He chuckled. "No, I'm quite sure she was where she said she was. The young girl seems awfully naïve, but I don't see a killer in her."

Nodding, Claire pressed on. "And what about Fiona? Ever figure out if she was at the garden centre the afternoon Nigella was poisoned?"

"Claims she was at a school meeting that afternoon." Ramsbottom scratched his hair with the end of his fork before using it to drive a wedge down the middle of the pie. "I spoke to the headmaster myself, and he wasn't sure of any meetings taking place, but he also was adamant that a meeting could have taken place. We have footage of her entering the school in the morning and leaving with the final bell, which should rule her out, but..." He stabbed one half of the pie and crammed it into his mouth. "It's not like the Deputy Headteacher teaches classes, and the school is surrounded by fields."

"So, she could have left?"

"It's a possibility we're trying to eliminate." Chewing his pie, he assessed Claire carefully. "She mentioned you turned up at her house under false pretences." She braced herself for her second authority scalding of the day. "Don't suppose she mentioned anything to you that rang alarm bells? I can't get a bead on her."

Claire glanced back at the booth, where Amelia and Hugo waited patiently.

"I did overhear her telling someone she loved them on the phone," Claire revealed. "Sounded like they might live in Portugal?"

"Hmm, I know her mum retired to Portugal a while back," Ramsbottom said. "She's always complaining on Facebook about how lonely she is. It could have been her on the other end of that phone call. How did the declaration of love sound to you?"

Casting her mind back to the overheard conversation on the day Sarah was poisoned, she tried to remember the tone. It replayed in her mind every which way.

"I'm not sure," she admitted.

He scooped up the last bite of pie and sat back with a

satisfied sigh. "Well, I'd best get back to it. Do try to stay out of things," he said, before adding in a lower voice, "but if you do hear anything, you know how to reach me."

With that, he lumbered off just as Ryan arrived.

"Good day at work?" Claire asked, joining him at the booth.

"Nailed the choreography in my boxercise class today," Ryan said with a smile. "How's everything here?"

"Oh, fine," Claire said breezily, not wanting to ruin the light-hearted mood with her late school confession; he must not have checked his phone yet. "Pool table is free. Who fancies a round before we leave?"

AT ALMOST MIDNIGHT, THE OLD SHED AT THE BOTTOM OF the garden creaked and groaned as a gust of wind swept over the dark garden. Claire pulled her mother's borrowed cardigan tighter, warding off the chill. The bare bulb cast deep shadows over her father's pensive face.

"Right then," Alan said briskly, rolling up his sleeves. "Let's go over everything we know about this puzzling case."

He began pinning notes, pictures, and documents back onto their investigation board, reassembling the complex web after the previous vandalism. Claire studied the familiar faces, hoping a solution might leap off the faded paper.

"Bernard seems the obvious choice to me," her father mused. "The invoices for foxglove plants were highly suspicious. And we know he was eager to push out Nigella to bring in commercial honey production."

Claire nodded slowly. "True. But that was just business to him. Would he really resort to murder over a stock dispute? He could have killed me for turning down his candle offer if that were his motive."

"Perhaps if he felt provoked enough for some other reason? Bernard has a bit of a temper." Alan tapped his chin with the end of his pen. "Did I mention I rang up an old friend from my detective days? He looked into the garden centre's history for me."

Leaning forward eagerly, Claire waited for him to continue.

"Turns out Bernard has a record of getting rather physical when frustrated," her father revealed. "About fifteen years back, shortly before Meadowview opened, Bernard got into a row with one of the builders of the place and ended up breaking the man's nose."

As mild-mannered as he tried to come across, Claire could easily imagine Bernard erupting in violence.

"Nothing so extreme since, but it could be telling," Alan concluded. "If Nigella kept thwarting his plans, it could have set him off."

"Hmm. He certainly had the means and opportunity. Would he still be strutting around the place so obviously if he were guilty?"

"A convincing actor, perhaps?" he suggested. "Either way, we can't rule him out yet."

Alan turned back to the board, his gaze landing on a grainy picture of Tom. "Financial adviser turned investor. He's made no secret that he intends to continue growing the business without Nigella. The question is, how far was Tom willing to go to claim his prize?"

A heavy silence hung between them. Claire knew they were both remembering those threatening honey jars. The vandalised evidence board. Someone dangerous and unhinged was still out there.

"At least we can rule out Hayley," Claire said after a moment. "Her grandmother and her baking buddies confirmed her alibi."

"And Sarah too, of course. We know now she's innocent."

Claire released a long breath. Given what Sarah had been through, she was confident they could strike her off the suspect list.

"Which leaves us with..." Her gaze landed on the last photo pinned up. "Fiona. The wife."

Alan nodded grimly. "Indeed. On the surface, she seemed above suspicion. But you've uncovered too many contradicting behaviours to ignore. The picture she painted of Nigella doesn't match what everyone else has said." He began ticking off points on his fingers. "Rushing to sell the house... siphoning away money... that mysterious phone caller she claimed to love."

Claire swallowed hard. "But do you really think she could have poisoned her own wife, estranged or not?"

"Desperation makes people capable of terrible things," he said, rubbing at the creases in his forehead as he leaned further into his chair. "If there's one thing my detective career taught me, it's that anyone can be pushed to become the worst version of themselves, given the right circumstances."

"The way I see it, we have three suspects," Claire said.

"Fiona, Tom, and Bernard," he agreed. "So, which of them saw Nigella as their ultimate obstacle, and why choose this moment to—"

Alan broke off as the shed door suddenly creaked open. Claire flinched, perched on her plant pot, her pulse racing. But it was only her mother in her quilted housecoat, clutching two steaming mugs.

"Brought you some Horlicks," she announced, holding out the drinks. "Thought you could use it, out here sleuthing half the night away. The weather's taken quite the turn."

"We're just reviewing the case, dear," Alan explained, blowing gently on the hot liquid before taking a sip.

Janet waved her hand dismissively. "Yes, yes, I know.

All this dreadful poisoning business." Her face softened, an uncommon vulnerability in her eyes. "That poor young waitress. I was too hard on her over that silly purse. If only..." she trailed off, shaking her head. "Well, no use dwelling on the past. I was thinking of offering Sarah a position with Janet's Angels, provided she can resist the temptation of other people's belongings in the future."

Claire nearly choked on her Horlicks. "You'd still give her a job after everything?"

"She's clearly got potential once she sorts out her priorities," Janet replied. Then her stern expression faltered. "She told the truth, and I've already forgiven her."

Even iron wills could bend, it seemed.

"Right, I'm off to bed. Don't stay up all night. It's only going to get colder."

"I think that's my cue as well," Claire stifled a yawn behind her hand. The day had drained her, and the warmth of the Horlicks was making her eyelids droop.

"I'll drive you home," Alan offered, levering himself up with his cane. "These dark streets are no place for a young woman alone."

Too tired to argue, Claire let him drive her across the shadowy cul-de-sac and down the lamp-lit lane into the village square. Her little flat above the shop beckoned invitingly. But as they drew near, Claire halted, the sight before her piercing through her weariness in an instant. Her heart stuttered.

The shop's front window, normally so pristine, was smeared with something sticky, catching the light in golden streaks. Dark shapes were stuck haphazardly across the glass.

"It's honey," Alan muttered. "Honey and foxgloves."

CHAPTER THIRTEEN

*C*ome morning, the sticky mess of honey and foxgloves was nothing but a bad memory. Although the police had kept watch outside her shop throughout the night, Claire was restless, tossing and turning until dawn. As she navigated the day in the shop on autopilot, the unsettling image from the previous evening gnawed at her, refusing to budge.

"This really might be your best candle yet," Eugene said near closing time, after a deep inhale of the star scent. "Our house has smelled exquisite all week, and even Marley hasn't complained about the fragrance in the air. Seeing this full display this morning has made me the happiest man in Northash."

"Glad to be of service," Claire said, keeping to herself that she was growing tired of the floral beeswax scent overwhelming the shop. "Not sure it can claim to be Nigella's final batch of wax anymore, but the murder tourists have eased off a little."

"Shame," Eugene loaded several jars into his basket. "You know, I still think you should put that recent front page in your window. I can't believe it's been a week since Nigella's murder, yet the culprit is still on the loose. I haven't taken my eyes off my cups all week."

Claire nodded grimly, not that she needed reminding. She'd awoken that morning with a lump in her throat when she'd realised the same. She looked to the window, and even though the glass now gleamed—courtesy of her mother's rigorous cleaning—Claire couldn't shake the illusion that golden smears of honey still marred the shop.

"Don't take this the wrong way, dear, but you look like you've been burning the candle at both ends," Eugene whispered as he settled the basket on the counter. "Late nights trying to solve the case, eh? Any hunches?"

Plenty for the café to gossip about, but nothing Claire wanted to share. Instead, she had a question for Eugene.

"You might be able to help me," Claire said, and he leaned in closer with an eager nod. "Noticed anyone in the café with strange rashes on their hands?"

"Foxglove rashes like the waitress has, you mean?" He chuckled. "DI Ramsbottom was just in the café asking the same thing to anyone who would listen. Quite desperate, if you ask me."

"Seems we've both reached the same dead-end."

"So, you *are* investigating?" Eugene's face lit up. "I'm sure you'll solve it before Ramsbottom because that man literally couldn't solve the easiest crossword clue in the paper this morning." He cleared his throat and said, "The surname of an amateur sleuth with a typewriter in Cabot Cove?"

"Fletcher."

"My point exactly," he toasted the paper bag to Claire after they finished the transaction. "And like Miss Fletcher, I'm sure you'll have the answers soon enough. Ramsbottom's focus seems to be on that waitress, thanks to her not being so truthful about some coffee beans, but she hardly poisoned herself, did she?"

Claire was disappointed that Ramsbottom was spreading the idea that Sarah could be guilty. If Ramsbottom was sharing case details openly, he must have been out of leads.

If the dose of poison Sarah had been slipped had been small, perhaps a case could have been built that she was trying to throw the investigation off her scent. But she'd spent days being kept alive by machines. Given that Sarah's misguided stealing indiscretions were in the name of providing for her children, Claire refused to believe she'd risk her life in such a way. She couldn't look after her children from behind prison bars or the afterlife. The pain on Sarah's face had been too genuine as she stared at her blistered hands.

There had to be someone else out there with a matching rash.

The sound of the coffee machine crunching through a fresh batch of beans drew Claire into the storeroom. Damon had finished adding labels to the stack of online orders Claire had boxed that afternoon, and he was slumping against the counter. Claire kicked the metal bin with a thud, and Damon bolted upright.

"What was your karaoke song this time?" she asked.

"It was actually *Dawn Ship 2* last night," he mumbled through a yawn. "I swear late nights didn't always feel like this. What happened?"

"You reached your mid-thirties?" Claire echoed his yawn and grabbed herself a cup as the machine finished dripping Damon's espresso. "But you're not the only one burning the candle at both ends. I barely slept."

"Wildflower worries?"

Claire nodded. She hadn't told Damon about the honey and foxglove attack. She didn't want him to spend the day worrying, and he hadn't noticed the police car that had been stationed outside the clock tower all day.

She took the lid off the empty sugar pot. She didn't mind her coffee as it came, but Damon couldn't stomach it without a little sweetness. With no spare bag in sight, she grabbed the jar of honey. Twisting open the jar, she stared at its splotchy surface.

"Weird," she said. "Does that look like mould to you?"

"Oh, gross. It does, but that should be impossible." Pushing up his glasses, he looked at Claire to see if he needed to explain. "There was a task on *Beekeeper Simulator 3* that led me to dig up a three-thousand-year-old pot of Egyptian honey. It was still fresh."

"In a video game."

"Okay, maybe the fact that I dug up the pot on my simulated farm and not in Egypt wasn't real. But then I fell down a rabbit hole reading Wiki pages," he said, checking to see if Claire was still listening. "Honey has low water content, high sugar, and an acidic pH. Bees produce their own hydrogen peroxide to fend off bacteria and fungi. It's basically nature's fortress."

"You're a bottomless well of information, Damon."

Claire lifted the honey jar up to the light. Tiny spores, like those on the surface, swirled around the amber liquid behind the 'MIND YOUR BEESWAX, BUSYBODY!' label still hanging from the rim.

"Could be poisoned?" Damon suggested.

"Not according to the police," she said, tightening the lid. "Maybe they contaminated it when they were taking their samples. Sorry, mate, you'll have to endure the full force of the beans."

"Whatever it takes to stop me from falling asleep in the cinema with Sally and the girls tonight."

Claire climbed the narrow staircase to her flat, leaving Damon to his rejuvenating coffee. She found Domino and Sid perched on the kitchen countertop, awaiting their dinner. She squeezed fresh pouches of food into their bowls and flicked on the television, setting it to their favourite twelve-hour video of birds jostling at a birdfeeder. Yet, as electronic chirps filled the room, her eyes fell upon another honey jar on the kitchen shelf. This was the one Nigella had given her in the candle exchange, left untouched since the unsettling events of the murder.

She held the jar up to the light. It was crystal clear, a far cry from the murky appearance of the one downstairs. Not only that, but the consistency was notably thicker—like liquid gold held captive in a jar. She'd noticed the mouldy jar had been suspiciously runnier when it first appeared as a threat on her doorstep.

The bell rattled below, pulling her attention back to the shop. With a promise to the cats that she'd be home later, she returned to the shop to find Hayley inspecting the suspicious jar of honey with Damon at the counter.

"Impossible," Hayley said.

Instinctively, Claire glanced down at Hayley's hands. No sign of a rash.

"I could offer you an exchange?" Hayley set down a box brimming with honey jars on the counter. "I've been delivering honey to our regular customers all afternoon. We have quite a few spares, and Tom wanted me to go door-to-door to see if anyone else would be interested. Don't suppose you'd want to add a new product line?"

"I'll have to think about it," Claire said, offering the politest smile she could muster for the frazzled-looking apprentice. "Couldn't you offer them to Bernard to sell at Meadowview?"

Hayley sighed. "That's what I suggested, but Tom's trying to negotiate a deal. Bernard's been offered cheaper factory-produced honey with his face plastered all over it, and now he doesn't want the competition." Staring at the box, a crease appeared between her brows, and she added, "We've never had this many leftover jars from a batch before, and this is before the new hives have started producing."

Claire exchanged a knowing look with Damon and said, "If the honey is spoiling, and there's more than usual that's not as thick as it used to be, could it have been watered down?"

Hayley's cheeks flushed as though embarrassed at the insinuation. "Adding water would... it would spoil it."

Glancing at the jars and then back to the honey, Claire didn't feel the need to say more.

"He wouldn't," Hayley said. "Tom wouldn't do that. He wouldn't ruin the batch for the sake of a few extra coins."

"What if he didn't know watering the honey down would ruin it?" Damon suggested. "He's a financial advisor, not a beekeeper."

"No. He's a good guy."

Claire sighed, recalling what Hayley had said about Nigella being in love with a version of Fiona that Hayley had never met. What version of Tom did Hayley know that Claire didn't?

"Bernard could be trying to sabotage us," Hayley suggested instead. "To get rid of our hives once and for all. I don't want to think he'd stoop that low, but he raised the rent again today. He was on the warpath." She offered Claire a tight smile. "How's your father doing?"

"Oh, he's fine," Claire replied. "Shouldn't he be?"

The bell tinkled, and Sally ushered her young daughters, Ellie and Aria, inside. Hayley stepped back from the counter, taking her jars of honey with her. Sally motioned to Damon and hung back by the door.

"Tom is a good guy," Hayley repeated in a quieter voice. "He's given me an opportunity to run a business, and it's not like I'm qualified for anything. If Nigella hadn't taught me everything she knows, I don't know what I'd be doing right now. When this loan comes through, I'm sure we'll be able to find a new site to set up our operation to continue what Nigella started."

That didn't sound like what Nigella had started at all.

"What loan?" Claire asked.

"I signed the paperwork for a business loan this morning," she said, glancing at the clock. "We should find out soon."

"Sorry, I couldn't help but overhear," Sally interjected as she joined them at the counter. "Did you just say you signed paperwork for a loan with Tom? Are you listed in the company paperwork?"

Hayley blushed, her shoulders hunching into a shrug.

"What did you sign, exactly? Did you read through it?"

"He said I didn't need to bother." Hayley's voice was shrinking with every word, her eyes fixed on the clock. "I need to get on with shifting these jars if we want to keep the hives where they are before we find somewhere else. The colony has been through enough this week."

Hayley hurried past the kids as they randomly pulled jars off the shelves. Sally's concerned glare followed Hayley to the door.

"What do you know that I don't?" Claire asked.

"We just had Tom in Smith and Smith practically begging us to ignore his failed credit checks and lack of deposit so he could rent somewhere. If he can't pass a credit check for a rental, he'll never pass one for a loan."

Claire didn't like the sound of where this was going. "Do you think he could be using Hayley to apply for a loan?"

"He seems to think he's more persuasive than he is." Sally rolled her eyes. "His reasoning for looking past his botched credit was laughable. Apparently, Smith and Smith making money from selling his sister's house means we must bow to his demands."

"Fiona didn't move estate agents then?"

Sally offered a dry smile. "I told you I was good at my job. Arranged five more viewings for her to smooth things over, and she accepted an offer from a family this afternoon. I'm going to drop off a bottle of champagne at Wordsworth Avenue on the way to the cinema to ensure I'm forgiven. She must be leaving soon if Tom is this desperate for somewhere to live. Speaking of which, Damon, we need to leave now if we want to get to the cinema on time."

"One more question," Claire called after Sally. "Did you notice if Tom had any strange rashes on his hands?"

Sally shook her head. "Rashes? Not that I noticed."

With Damon and Sally heading to the cinema, Claire locked up the shop for the evening. A sense of urgency gnawed at her as she made her way to the quiet cul-de-sac. She needed her father's wisdom to unravel the mystery that loomed over them. With Fiona's abrupt departure to Portugal and Tom's hasty plans to expand and relocate Nigella's passion project, solving the case was slipping through their fingers like a bad batch of watered-down honey.

CHAPTER FOURTEEN

*C*laire let herself into her parents' house, the familiar scent of roast dinner filling the air. She'd expected to find her mum, Janet, rushing about the kitchen, but instead, she was greeted by the innocent giggles of Amelia and Hugo wafting from the sitting room. Curiosity piqued, she tiptoed closer.

Peering around the doorframe, Claire found a heart-warming scene that caught her off guard. Ryan and the kids were snuggled up on the sofa, captivated by what appeared to be old home videos flickering on the TV screen. Sitting apart from them was her father, perched on his favourite armchair. His smile was uncharacteristically broad, stretching from ear to ear.

"What's all this then?" Claire finally announced her

presence, her eyes dancing from one happy face to another.

Ryan looked up and beckoned her over. "I was just returning these old tapes that your dad lent me a few weeks back."

"His mum's in them," Alan explained, eyes still on the screen. "Feels so long ago, and yet I can't believe so much time has passed."

Intrigued, Claire realised these must have been the attic VHS tapes that inspired her father to start working at Meadowview.

Taking her place on the arm of the sofa beside Amelia, Claire was drawn into the footage. Younger versions of herself and Ryan were on the screen, kicking a football around in an open field. Their youthful faces were flushed from running and laughter. Alan was in one goal, Paula—Ryan's late mother—in another. Behind the camera, no doubt, was Janet.

"Why does your hair look like that?" Amelia asked as the camera focused on Claire's face and her short, choppy fringe. "Looks funny."

"You can thank my mother's kitchen scissor haircuts for that." Young Claire grinned at the camera, showing off a gummy smile, missing several teeth. "If Janet ever tells you she's read an article on how to cut hair and knows what she's doing, run."

"Do you remember this day?" Ryan glanced at her, his eyes searching for shared nostalgia.

Claire shook her head gently. "Can't say that I do. But we sure look happy, don't we?"

Hugo, who had been riveted by the screen, suddenly piped up. His tiny finger pointed to Paula, defending her goal from Claire's awkward dribbling. "Is that our other grandma?"

Ryan nodded, a melancholy edge tinting his smile.

The video reached its end, the screen going blank. Alan sprang to life and turned the TV off.

"C'mon, you two rascals. I need some help peeling potatoes."

As the room emptied, Claire felt the shift in the atmosphere. Ryan's smile faded, and it must have been for the benefit of the kids. He hadn't mentioned he'd had these tapes, but Claire suspected they might have contributed to his recent shift in his mood.

"I miss her too, you know," she ventured softly, observing Ryan's eyes fixated on the blank screen. "Paula was an incredible mum."

Ryan's face softened. "Yeah, she was. She always made sure I had everything I needed, even when times were tough. I don't know how she did it and made it look so easy."

"It probably wasn't easy," Claire said. "We were just

kids who didn't know how the world worked. It wasn't all summer days running around playing football."

"I just don't know how I'll ever live up to her." Before Claire could offer any reassurances, Ryan shifted gears. "I need to step up and build a better life for the kids. I thought moving back to Northash after everything fell apart, I'd be able to give them the childhood I had, but... I don't know where I'm going wrong, Claire."

"Who said you're going wrong, Ryan?"

"I've been thinking a lot about that manager job in Burnley," he said, Claire's words not making a difference. "I keep staring at the online ad, questioning why I haven't applied yet. It's a good opportunity. Better pay. I could save up. Move the kids somewhere with a garden. We could go on holiday. I wouldn't have to worry when their school uniforms start to look too small, or the price of food goes up again."

"You'd be happy commuting forty minutes every day?" Claire asked. "Each way."

"I'd do what I had to."

"But what about the time you'd lose with the kids? Or the time for things that make you, well, you? Painting..." Claire paused, almost saying 'me' but didn't want to make it about herself. "I don't think you've thought this through."

Ryan's eyes tightened, and his voice sharpened ever so

slightly. "I'm just trying to do what's best for my family, Claire. You wouldn't understand."

His words, soft as they were, felt like a gut punch. Claire withdrew her hand from his, feeling the itch of the sting.

Before she could respond, the piercing sound of squealing tires shattered the calm of the cul-de-sac outside. Exchanging a bewildered look with Ryan, Claire went to see who could have arrived in such a state. She opened the door to a red-faced, breathless Bernard on the doorstep. His eyes blazed as he scanned past Claire into the house.

"Where's Alan?" Bernard demanded. "I need to speak to him. *Now.*"

Claire blocked his path with her arm. "First, you need to calm down. What's this about?"

Bernard jabbed an accusing finger at her. "*Calm down?* I just spent days in a cell wondering what the police could have on me. I did some of my own digging and found out it was all thanks to your father sticking his nose where it doesn't belong. The fool twisted the ear of his old buddy and almost had me charged with murder."

Alan hobbled from the kitchen, shutting the kids inside.

"Better come in, Bernard," he said wearily. "We can talk this through like civilized adults, or not at all."

With simmering anger, Bernard pushed past Claire,

and she shut the front door. Claire ducked into the kitchen as her father led Bernard into the sitting room.

"Who was that man?" Amelia asked, pausing in her enthusiastic potato peeling efforts.

"Nobody to worry about," Claire reassured her as Ryan gathered the kids' things to leave.

"I should get these two home," he muttered. "Good luck with..."

He tipped his head towards the raised voices.

"You're not staying for dinner?" she asked.

"I'll grab something on the way home," he said, waving for the kids to leave the kitchen. "I'll see you later."

Claire nodded, feeling another pang as Ryan rushed the kids out the front door without so much as a proper goodbye. With a resigned sigh, she busied herself filling the kettle, though her hands shook slightly. She couldn't get Ryan's words out of her head.

You wouldn't understand.

Each word felt like a needle pricking her skin.

Of course, she understood wanting the best for his children. She loved those kids. But she also knew there was no magic bullet—no high-paying job or a big house with a garden—that would solve everything in an instant. Sacrifices always had to be made.

She thought back to her own childhood in the cul-de-sac. Growing up in the comfortable middle, she'd never felt like she was missing out, her problems more with her fussy mother's judgment or school bullies. And she'd had Ryan by her side, always there to listen and join her in a scheme.

Maybe she didn't fully understand Ryan's struggles as a single parent. But she wanted to. She wanted to support him, to lift some of that burden from his shoulders. She thought she'd been trying to. These past weeks, she'd only caught glimpses of the old Ryan from the tapes before life got to him. She was losing him again, different than last time. She had to find a way to bridge that gap before it was too late. To make him see that she was on his side.

If her mother hadn't stumbled upon these tapes, the Nigella case might've just been a fleeting headline she'd seen in the paper—nothing more. Ryan might not have been reminded of how different his life in Northash was now compared to the rose-tinted summer days he remembered before all those years away.

She remembered why she was at the cul-de-sac and carried the tray into the sitting room. Bernard was pacing in front of the TV while Alan sat in his armchair, hands clasped together.

"I promise you, I had nothing to do with Nigella's death," Bernard insisted. "But you just had to keep digging, didn't you?"

Alan held up a hand. "Please, sit down and let's discuss this properly."

With a huff, Bernard dropped onto the sofa while Claire handed out mugs.

"Now," her father began calmly, "why don't you explain why you believe I'm responsible for your arrest?"

Bernard took a long gulp of tea before speaking. "After those thefts started at the garden centre, I installed security cameras in my office. I caught you red-handed snooping around in there, going through my paperwork and emails."

"I admit I was looking for any information that might be relevant to the case," her father confessed. "With Nigella's poisoning, it seemed prudent to investigate all angles."

"*Prudent?*" Bernard slammed his mug down. "My factory contracts and foxglove invoices aren't evidence in a murder case. They're my private business dealings."

"Well, I did think they seemed rather incriminating given—"

"Of course *you* did! And you went straight to the police to point the finger at me instead of asking me about it. But I've done nothing wrong."

Lingering behind the sofa, Claire decided she couldn't stand by and listen to Bernard shouting around in circles all night.

"You *did* order large amounts of foxglove plants," she pointed out. "Right before Nigella died from foxglove poisoning. And you *were* trying to push Nigella out so you could work with the honey factory instead."

"The foxgloves were for restocking!" Bernard cried in exasperation. "We were short on several flower varieties because someone messed up with the seeding earlier in the year. You'd have noticed many invoices if you hadn't been focused in on the foxgloves. And yes, I wanted to expand honey production, but that's not a crime. Nigella refused to increase production to meet my stock requirements, prattling on about organic, small-batch methods. So, I found another provider who could meet higher demand. That's just business sense. I didn't kill the blasted woman over it."

While frustrating to hear, Bernard's impassioned denials carried an air of truth. At best, the evidence against him was incidental, and his delivery of the supposed motive made it seem even less credible.

"Bernard, I apologise for any trouble caused," Alan said, standing and stretching out a hand. "I may have been overzealous in my speculations."

With a disgruntled huff, Bernard straightened his jacket, ignoring the hand. Alan left it there for a moment before dropping it to his side.

"Well, I hope you'll avoid any further baseless accusations against me," Bernard said. "And unless you're there to buy something, I don't want to see you at the garden centre again."

"I take it that means I've been fired?"

"Very perceptive," he muttered, glaring at Claire as he walked to the hallway. "I'll see myself out."

The front door slammed behind Bernard as he left. Claire was glad he'd gone, but his strange energy still lingered.

"Do you really think he's innocent?" she asked, breaking the silence.

Alan spread his hands helplessly. "I'm not sure what to think anymore. But attacking him further without proof won't help matters. We need to refocus our efforts."

Their quest for answers seemed to have reached another dead end. As dusk deepened outside, they trudged to the shed to pore over their investigation board, hoping desperately for some small breakthrough. But when Alan pushed open the door, they were met with a disheartening sight.

Their carefully assembled web of photos, notes, and speculations had been viciously vandalised again, with angry red letters scrawled across the board reading 'LEAVE IT ALONE!' Another jar of honey had also been left on the worktable, and the ominous message read: 'BUZZ OFF. FINAL WARNING.'

Claire felt the last shreds of patience snap. Grabbing the jar, she marched outside and hurled it violently against the garden fence. It shattered in a viscous, sticky explosion, flecks of honey splattering the patio tiles.

Chest heaving, she turned to find her father watching her with concern from the doorway.

"What is it, love?" he asked gently. "What's really going on?"

Claire felt furious, tears threatening to spill over. "I just don't know how to do this, Dad. The shop, Ryan, the kids, this bloody case—it's all getting too much. I'm trying, but..."

She trailed off, taking a shaky breath and swiping angrily at her eyes. Alan stepped forward and folded her into a hug. For once, it didn't make everything go away. Claire recounted their strained conversation from earlier: Ryan's concerns about providing for the kids, his comment that she didn't understand, her growing sense that he was slipping away.

"Those tapes," Claire said, her voice muffled against his shoulder, "I think they might have sent Ryan into the spiral Mum thought they'd send you into. He seems to think he's failing the kids because he's not giving them the same childhood his mum gave him."

"Ah, I see." Alan inhaled and pulled away, offering a tight smile. "Seems he's caught the nostalgia bug. That wasn't my intention when I gave him those tapes. You know, Paula struggled too." He exhaled and glanced at the dark house next door. "After Ryan's dad left, becoming a single parent wasn't an easy transition for her. I can't tell you how many nights Janet and I lent her a listening ear over that fence. She thought we had it all figured out because there were two of us to look after you." He chuckled and shook his head. "Which is funny because I used to wish to be more like her. Home all the time, getting by selling her art. Oh, how I wish I'd been retired during those years. I felt like I missed so much of your childhood."

"That's not how it felt to me," Claire said.

"Because I always tried to make the time I was there count. But when I look back, I'm sure I see something very different from what you see," he said. His gaze drifted off into the distance. "I remember too many difficult days hunched over desks in dark offices. Restless nights spent trying to piece together impossible clues. The desperation to climb the career ladder to give you everything I never had. Moments of joy at home were just peppered around the edges. I felt a similar burden to what I think Ryan's feeling now. The need to provide." He cupped Claire's cheek in his worn palm. "In a perfect world, my memories would all be about playing goalkeeper and trying to defend your hair from your mum's kitchen scissors."

They shared a laugh, and Claire was glad she'd confided in her father.

"When Ryan left their life in Spain," he continued, "I'm sure he thought he was setting sail back to the grainy VHS days of his childhood. But your Uncle Pat's old place is a far cry from this cul-de-sac. And yet," he paused, casting another glance at the empty house next door, "when Amelia and Hugo look back on these years, they won't see a lack of middle-class suburbia. They'll see a dad who's obviously trying his best. But no matter what, one day Ryan will look back with regrets about his choices."

"I want to be there for him and the kids. I'm not their mum, but I want what's best for them," Claire said. "I've bonded with them."

"Then you understand Ryan's conflict. But the hard truth is, we don't always know what's best until we've made the mistakes," he said, exhaling up at the darkening sky. "I could have taken fewer cases and worked fewer weekends. Sarah could have left the coffee beans and your mum's purse alone. Fiona could have married someone who wanted the same future. Bernard could have left that man's nose unbroken and treated his staff better. Tom could have found a willing business partner." Alan paused, locking eyes with Claire and tilting his head slightly—a silent nudge for her to absorb his words. "Ryan may think providing in this way is best for now. But if you think he's about to make a wrong turn, you're the one who can get through to him."

"And if it's too late?"

"You get your worrying from your mother," he said, offering a dry smile. "If Ryan is the man I think he is, he'll be reflecting on how your conversation could have gone differently. The dust will settle, and you and your found family will have brighter days ahead."

Claire managed a small, grateful smile. Her dad always knew what to say.

"Thanks, Dad," Claire said, wiping away tears. "How did you get so wise?"

"I lived it," he said, giving her arm a reassuring squeeze. "Difficult days like these teach us the most. Now, let's focus on what we can control." He stamped his cane down on a stepping stone. "If we take Bernard at his word, our suspect list has narrowed to two troubled siblings who just happen to live together. It's time to pay Tom and Fiona a visit."

Taking a deep, steadying breath, Claire linked her arm through her father's. As much as this case had become a frustrating distraction, he was right. She'd let the situation with Ryan settle until morning. She needed a restful night's sleep, but after the abstract honey art on her shop window and another attack on their shed, she needed answers first. With renewed determination, they set off down the stepping stones back to the house.

CHAPTER FIFTEEN

They arrived at Wordsworth Avenue, but Fiona's house was the only dark one on the street. Nobody was home. Claire wondered if they were too late, and Fiona had already fled to Portugal. And who knew where Tom could be lurking? The street was eerily silent, not even a dog barking or leaves rustling, just the faint whistle of wind through the darkness.

"Well, which of them do you think did it?" her father asked, peering up at the lifeless windows.

Claire bit her lip, hesitating. There was something sinister about Tom trying to profit off his sister-in-law's misery. The way he was pushing to expand the business, potentially watering down the honey, talks of a loan... and he'd threatened Claire the last time she'd visited Wordsworth Avenue.

But Fiona had lied about Nigella's character, portraying her as selfish and obsessed in a way that didn't fit with anything else Claire had heard. Fiona had described a woman Claire didn't recognise—and she'd done it so smoothly, like slipping on a mask. Why twist the truth if not to make Nigella look worse and cast herself in a better light?

Before Claire could respond, headlights flashed behind them. She whirled around, half-expecting to see Tom's beat-up Land Rover pulling onto the street. But it was another familiar car. Sally and Damon climbed out, laughing about something. Their cheer faded as they approached and noticed Claire and her dad lurking outside the dark house.

"Claire?" Sally squinted into the dark. "What are you doing here?"

"I could ask you the same."

"I forgot to drop off Fiona's champagne earlier," Sally said, hoisting up a bottle. "I was going to leave it on the step with a little note. What are you two doing here?"

"We think we've narrowed it down to one of the siblings," Alan explained. "Bernard is a pain, but doesn't seem like a killer."

"And Sarah didn't poison herself," Claire said. "It must be one of these two. We thought they might slip up if we could talk to them. But we might be too late. Fiona might be on a Portuguese beach right now, and Tom could be anywhere."

"Would a final poke around inside help?" Sally began rifling through her massive handbag, tongue poking from the corner of her mouth in concentration. "Because it's your lucky day..." She plucked out a jumble of keys. "I have the spare."

Alan cleared his throat. "Now, Sally, I appreciate your intentions, but we can't let ourselves into a client's home without permission. That would be breaking the law. I may be retired, but we're not stepping over that line."

"But I have permission." Sally waved the keys breezily, undeterred by his ethical concerns. "I'm simply providing you all a quick private showing, that's all. In case the sale falls through. Can't be too careful these days with deals collapsing left and right." She darted her brows up and down, spinning the keyring around on her finger. "So, who's up for a viewing?"

"You scare me sometimes, Sal," Damon said. "Why do I like it?"

Looking impressed with herself, Sally dug amongst the keys, checking the labels.

"Alright, here's what we'll do," Alan finally relented with a sigh. "I'll stay out here and keep watch with the girls. You all keep your eyes peeled through the windows. I'll flash the headlines if you need to make a quick exit. Got it?"

Sally selected the right key, and Claire felt a thrill of trepidation as they pushed open the door. Half-packed boxes lay strewn about in a state of disarray, their contents spilling out like exposed secrets. Photo albums gaped open on the floor, their walls stripped of the frames that once held happier times. The house seemed suspended in a moment of flight, as if its inhabitants had paused their packing, poised to escape but not quite ready to leave. An odd sensation crept up Claire's spine, a feeling that they could be moments from finding something that could point them in the right direction.

"What exactly are we looking for?" Damon's voice sliced through the quiet, louder than he probably intended, snapping Claire back to reality.

"Clues, genius. Evidence," Sally hissed, scanning the room warily as if expecting someone to leap from the shadows. "If this was one of your games, where would you search first?"

Damon perked up, snapping his fingers. "I'd scour every nook and cranny until I uncovered something vital to progress the investigation." He nodded, psyching himself up. "I'll start with the kitchen."

Tiptoeing, Damon scurried down the hall. Claire winced as a floorboard creaked under his Converse. So much for stealth.

Meanwhile, Sally was already creeping her way upstairs, one hand trailing along the wall to guide herself in the dark. Claire watched her silhouette disappear onto the second floor before turning her attention back to the living room.

Her gaze was drawn to the large wedding portrait still hanging over the mantel. Nigella and Fiona looked so vibrant, joyful, oblivious to the painful divergence of their lives to come. Had that happy-looking couple really grown apart into bitter strangers? Were they ever truly happy or just blinded by love?

Would Claire think that looking back on this past year with Ryan one day? Shaking her head, she wouldn't let her mind go there.

She scanned the room by moonlight filtering through the curtains. She noticed a photo album had been left open atop a crowded bookshelf. Crouching down, she carefully flipped through pages of Nigella and Fiona smiling and embracing in foreign airports, tourist spots around Europe, and sunny beaches.

In the earliest pictures, Fiona looked different—more carefree and bohemian, often adorned in flowy dresses or ripped jeans. The polished, reserved woman Claire had met recently seemed different altogether.

On the other hand, Nigella appeared identical from her wedding day through to the bitter end: kind-eyed, purposeful, in clothes at home among trees and creatures. She'd deserved someone who understood her passions, Claire thought, not someone delivering ultimatums against them. If only Nigella could've moved on and found real happiness.

After scanning the photo album filled with happy memories, Claire left it on the sofa and continued searching the living room. However, she found nothing else of interest among the strewn, packed boxes and hastily covered furniture.

With a frustrated sigh, she moved to the dining room, where Damon was perusing a book he'd taken from the built-in shelves.

"Find anything good?" Claire asked.

"Maybe," Damon replied. He held up the book so she could see the cover: 'Wildflowers of the British Countryside.' "Look familiar?"

Claire's brow furrowed. It was identical to her father's reference guide in his garden shed. She stepped closer as Damon flicked through the pages until the book landed at a natural point—an entry on foxglove plants. Someone had folded over the corner of the toxic wildflower.

Damon let out a low whistle. "Would be a crazy coincidence."

"I don't think it's a coincidence at all."

Before they could discuss it further, Sally came barrelling down the stairs in a panic.

"Who was on lookout?" she cried in a hushed voice.

Damon slapped the book shut and shoved it back on the shelf just as Claire glimpsed her dad's flashing headlines through the window. Frantically, she gestured for them to get down. Sally sprang into action, shoving them toward the back of the house.

"Go, go, *go!*" she urged, her voice strained. "The patio doors!"

But Claire froze halfway across the living room, her gaze fixed on the open photo album she'd left on the sofa. "They'll know someone was here."

She lunged for it, but Sally and Damon were already grabbing her arms, dragging her onward.

"I could lose my job, Claire!" Sally begged, near tears now. "Just run, I'm begging you!"

"You'll lose your job if they figure it out. How many people have spare keys?"

With no time left to argue, Claire wrenched herself free and dashed back as she heard the patio doors slide shut. Fumbling in the dark, she put the album back on the shelf she'd found it seconds before a key rattled in the front door.

She dropped to the floor, crawling behind the sheet-covered sofa, struggling to calm her ragged breathing as two figures entered the hallway. Claire squeezed her eyes shut, her heartbeat hammering in her ears. This was it. She was trapped.

"Just go and pack your things," came Fiona's drained voice.

"And where exactly am I supposed to go?" Tom

demanded.

"I don't care. Figure it out. You're a grown man, Tom."

Grumbling under his breath, Tom stomped upstairs, each footstep making Claire flinch. She held her breath as Fiona walked further into the house, terrified she'd be discovered any second.

Instead, a moment later, she heard the soft beeps of Fiona dialling her phone in the kitchen. Pressing deeper into the shadows, Claire strained to listen.

"Hey Mum, it's me," Fiona murmured. "No, he's not coming anymore." A heavy sigh. "I don't know. He'll sort something out. I told you, I need a fresh start..."

A fresh start. The words pierced Claire's heart. She thought of the heartache in Fiona's voice when she'd confessed her failed marriage dreams. But did a fresh start mean fleeing the country without consequences?

"Okay, I love you too," Fiona said softly after a pause. "See you at the airport tomorrow."

Claire tensed as the lights suddenly flashed on in the living room, searing through her closed eyelids. This was it. She was busted. She held her breath, bracing herself to be dragged out from her hiding spot at any second.

But to her shock, Fiona's footsteps moved away again after an agonizing moment, flipping the lights back off. Letting out a shaky breath, Claire remained frozen until she heard the soft gurgle of Fiona filling a glass with water in the kitchen.

Claire scrambled on all fours to the patio doors as soon as she was certain the coast was clear. After fumbling unsuccessfully for the handle in the dark, she finally slid the door open and slipped outside into the chilly night air.

Her heart still racing, she scanned the shadowy backyard until she noticed two pale faces peering down at her from the treehouse window. Sally and Damon. Claire picked her way across the lawn, her shoes dampening with dew.

"What happened?" Damon whispered urgently as they descended the ladder. "We thought for sure..." He mimed a throat being slit dramatically.

Sally rolled her eyes before turning to Claire, her lips pursed tight. "Are you okay?"

Claire nodded, still trying to catch her breath and slow her racing heart as they hurried down the side of the house. But then she noticed Sally scratching at her palms, and Claire recoiled at an angry red rash marring her skin.

It was unmistakable.

"Sally, did you touch any plants upstairs?"

"Plants?" Sally shook her head, wincing as she examined the inflamed sores she couldn't stop scratching. "No, nothing like that. I was rifling through things on Tom's desk. Boring stuff. Some stationery, business letters, teabags, socks—"

"Teabags?" Claire repeated. Dread swirled inside her. "What kind of teabags exactly?"

"I don't know. Normal everyday teabags?"

Exchanging an ominous look with Damon, Claire took Sally's arm and led her around the side of the house toward the street. They had to get her away from here and figure out what was happening.

Her father sat waiting in the idling car, neck craned toward the house. Relief flooded his features when he spotted them.

"Thank heavens!" Alan breathed as they scrambled inside.

"Step on it, Dad!"

"I can't drive this," he said, slapping his bad leg. "My foot. I drive an automatic."

"I can't drive right now," Sally said, wringing her hands in the back seat.

"Claire, lend me your leg," he said. "I know you failed your driving test three times, but I need you to put your foot down on the clutch."

"Not to panic anyone," Damon whispered, "but there's someone at the front door."

Claire reached her leg into the driver's side footwell and looked to the door as a silhouette appeared, backlit at the house on the corner of Wordsworth Avenue. She pressed down on the clutch, and Alan started the engine.

Tires squealed as they peeled away down the shadowy street in jittery spurts.

In the backseat, Sally frantically scrubbed at her inflamed hands with antiseptic wipes, wincing in pain. Claire's heart ached for her friend, wishing she'd warned her to stay away from any mysterious-looking teabags.

"You'll be okay," Alan reassured Sally, meeting her frightened eyes in the rear-view mirror. "Some antihistamines and some hydrocortisone cream and you'll be on the mend. Just don't scratch, whatever you do."

Claire's mind raced as she turned over this new chilling development. A risky but clear plan was already sparking in her mind, coming to her as quickly as the formula for her wildflower beeswax candles had.

"I think I know what's going on now," she said with dark determination. "Fiona's leaving the country tomorrow night, so we'll need to move quickly. We're going to bring everything tumbling down... with a nice soothing cup of tea."

SALLY'S CAR DROVE OFF INTO THE NIGHT AS CLAIRE AND her father crept across the deserted car park, their shoes crunching on gravel. The silvery moon hung above like a ghostly eye, casting an eerie shadow over Meadowview. In the distance, a siren wailed, its lonely cry fading into the darkness. Somewhere nearby, an owl hooted. She rubbed her arms, wondering where the spring heat had gone.

"Remind me why we're here again?" her father whispered.

"I just want to check something." Claire crept up to the locked front doors and cupped her hands around her eyes, peering through the glass. Not a breath of life stirred in the normally bustling garden centre. "What's the quickest way to the hives without cutting through?"

"This way."

They made their way around the large glass structure, sticking close to the building's side until they reached the hives. The air vibrated with the low hum of the bees, hard at work even at this late hour.

"We shouldn't disturb them," Alan warned.

"We're not going to." Claire's eyes were fixed on scanning the back of the building. "Where's the café in relation to here?"

Alan considered the question as he traced his mental map of Meadowview.

"Just around that corner," he said, jutting his cane ahead. "But there's no way in from the outside."

Claire set off anyway, and after some rustling through the bushes, she found what she was looking for: a substantial green fire escape door. Given the café's window placement, it led where she suspected.

"There had to be a covert way in," she told her father in an excited whisper. "This'll open into the kitchen, won't it?"

After some more consideration, Alan nodded.

"Both times, the deadly brew was left to steep unattended in the kitchen," she explained. "A simple teabag added to a cup, but they didn't go through the café, did they? They would have been seen."

"But without a key, this door only opens from the inside."

"And what did Bernard say about his missing keys?" Claire reminded him. "The thief and the poisoner are one and the same, and tomorrow, they'll let themselves in through this door one last time."

Leaving Meadowview, Claire steeled her nerves by gazing up at the dark silhouette of the candle factory as they made their way back towards the village. No matter the risk, she would lay her trap to bring Nigella's cold-blooded killer to long-awaited justice. The time had come to end this.

Once they were under the shade of The Canopies, her father asked, "So, what's our next move in this scheme of yours?"

"You're not going to like this," Claire said, looking him firmly in the eye, "but tomorrow, I'm going to order a cup of tea at the garden centre café, and there *will* be poison in it."

Claire released a tired sigh as she entered her flat, kicking off her shoes and placing her bag down, the weight of the day settling on her shoulders.

The living room basked in lamplight, and Claire was surprised to find Ryan lounging on her sofa, flipping through a fitness magazine. He glanced up at her and offered a tentative smile.

"Hey," he said, straightening and tossing the magazine onto the coffee table. "I hope you don't mind me letting myself in."

Claire moved to join him on the couch. "Of course not. That's why I gave you a key. Are the kids here?"

Ryan nodded towards the spare bedroom. "Out like lights already. Long day." He studied her face for a moment, his expression serious. "Listen, I owe you an apology for earlier. What I said about you not understanding..." He rubbed the back of his neck awkwardly. "That was out of line. I'm sorry."

Claire waved a hand, the tightness in her chest easing just a bit. "It's okay, Ryan. I know you've got a lot on your plate right now."

"Doesn't make it alright." Ryan reached for her hand,

his thumb brushing over her knuckles. "Amelia and Hugo gave me a talking to about it after I took them home. They realised something was wrong after our quick exit. They're good kids. Don't know what I did to deserve them."

Claire smiled, squeezing his hand. "Well, they clearly learned compassion from you."

Ryan's expression turned serious again. "Amelia also told me about what happened at school with her drawings. She must have overheard us talking." Looking pained, he scrubbed a hand down his face. "I never wanted them worrying about any of this. Seeing those videos, how perfect things were—"

"Things weren't perfect," Claire interrupted. "I might not remember that specific day, but I remember much more about that time than cul-de-sac football. Like how torn up you were about your dad leaving, how mean kids were to you at school. And I'm sure it wasn't all a breeze for your mum, either."

He smiled. "You're right. You're always right, Claire. And you were right earlier. If I worked further away, I'd have less time for them. I already knew that. I've been working more lately to cover the bills, but that makes me feel guilty for not being around enough. I feel guilty that you're picking up the slack. It's like I can't win. I want what's best for them."

"And sometimes, we don't always know what's best

until we've made the mistakes," she said, her lips curving into a smile at echoing her father's earlier wisdom. "You're under a lot of pressure right now juggling responsibilities, but... I don't think they want more. Every kid wants a big garden and a treehouse on some quiet fancy street, but that stuff means nothing without the love to go with it, and you give them that in spades. There are people much worse off, like Sarah in that tiny flat working for pennies. But there are also people in big houses who are lonely, like Fiona. If you asked the kids to choose between more money for a bigger house or staying where they were but having more time with their dad, I know what they'd choose."

Ryan's expression softened, some of the strain leaving his broad shoulders. "How is it you always know just what to say?" he asked, a hint of wonder in his voice that made Claire's cheeks warm happily.

"Because I know you," she said. "And I want the best for you... and for us." She glanced at the closed bedroom door. "If applying for that manager's position in Burnley is what you want, we'll make it work, but I don't think you need to."

"I might need to," he admitted in a whisper. "I sent a text message to the gym owner before the kids calmed me down. I told him that if I was good enough to be a temporary manager, I was good enough for the real thing, at the proper wage."

"And?"

"He hasn't replied," he said. "There are other jobs in Northash, I suppose. I trained to be a personal trainer, and it's not too late to retrain. Could always ask Sally about becoming an estate agent, and the candle factory always has jobs going."

She opened her mouth to tell him it wouldn't come to that just as her stomach let out an embarrassingly loud growl. She clamped her mouth shut, feeling her face flush.

Ryan laughed, the tender mood shifting. "You make a valid point, monster in Claire's stomach."

Claire swatted his arm playfully, joining in his laughter. "I never did get around to eating dinner tonight."

"Well, we can't have that. How about I pop out and grab us a pizza?"

"You don't have to."

But Ryan already had his keys out. "The usual?"

Claire nodded, touched by his thoughtfulness. As Ryan headed for the door, she called, "Don't forget the garlic knots."

The shop door clicked shut downstairs as Claire made her way to the kitchen to prep the plates. Mid-stride, she remembered the cans of toffee apple cider chilling in the fridge. Hand hovering over the handle, she paused. A fresh Amelia Tyler creation was nestled beneath fridge magnets next to the vibrant foxglove drawing. It showcased Claire with a magnifying glass, intently studying an array of wildflowers. Across the top, in Amelia's best handwriting, read 'World's Best Detective.'

A smile spread across Claire's face.

Like Nigella, Claire had been sure she hadn't wanted children. She hadn't considered herself to have any maternal instincts. But these days? The thought of life without Amelia and Hugo seemed unimaginable. Replacing their mother was out of the question—even if Maya was out of the picture—but Claire did feel like something to them.

Step-mum, parental figure, dad's girlfriend, World's Best Detective, or just 'Claire'—the label held little weight.

As she grabbed the cider cans and closed the fridge, her eye caught the jar of Nigella's honey perched on the counter. A snippet of an earlier conversation resurfaced. Nigella had mentioned something intriguing during their tour of the beehives, something she hadn't thought much about. With thoughts of 'replacements' still dancing in her mind, a light bulb flicked on.

Perhaps the queen bee had unwittingly trained her successor.

And just like that, the final pieces slid into place.

CHAPTER SIXTEEN

he sun beamed down on a perfect spring morning as Claire strolled through the garden centre, weaving between overflowing flower beds and potted trees. She spotted her father chatting with Bernard near the rows of vegetable seedlings. Deep in discussion, Bernard's expression hinted at disbelief, but he appeared in a much better mood than yesterday. Her father's eyes briefly met hers, and he offered a light nod.

Operation 'Poison Claire's Tea' was in motion.

Claire meandered through the flowerbeds and out through the back door. The comforting hum of the beehives grew nearer, and Claire quickened her pace. She found Hayley where she expected, tending to the active hives with gentle puffs of smoke, the bees buzzing lazily around her.

"Morning, Hayley," Claire called as she approached.

The former apprentice jumped, nearly dropping the smoker. "Claire, you startled me." She let out an embarrassed laugh, tucking back a loose strand of hair that had escaped her braid. "Did you change your mind about stocking our honey in your shop?"

"I'm afraid not," she said. "Not with your current business structure, at least."

Claire moved closer, and she could see the dark circles smudging the girl's eyes and the sag in her slender shoulders. She looked beyond drained. Claire's heart went out to her, knowing who was responsible for running the sweet girl ragged.

"How're things going?"

Hayley managed a weak smile. "Oh, you know. Same old. Tom's got me going from sun up to sun down most days. I'm just checking the brood boxes before the next harvest. The queen's been laying quite a lot recently. Claire, can I show…"

Her voice disappeared with the smoke.

"What is it?"

Hayley hesitated, chewing her lip. After a moment, she pulled out her mobile, scrolling through to show Claire an email open on the screen.

"Seems you and your friend were right to be sceptical about that business loan stuff," she admitted in a small voice. "I was sent this email this morning telling me *my* loan application was rejected. Unless Tom got things mixed up, I—"

"I think Tom did exactly what he intended to," Claire interrupted with a supportive smile. "And I'm sorry you got caught up in his swarm. This rejection is a blessing in disguise."

"We do need to increase profits if we want to stay here." Looking uncertain, Hayley tucked her phone away again. "I can't just abandon Nigella's bees. She trusted me to care for them."

Claire nodded, but she wasn't there to talk about the future of the hives. She was there to lay the past to rest, and she needed Hayley's help to put the plan into action.

"Hayley, can I ask for a favour?"

The girl eyed her curiously. "What kind of favour?"

"I need you to call Tom," Claire said, a quiver in her voice. "I need you to call Tom and tell him I showed up here demanding to see him and saying strange things about him that don't make sense before storming off. When he asks where I went, tell him you don't know, but you overheard me say I'll meet someone in the café at half-past two."

TWENTY MINUTES LATER, CLAIRE FOUND HER FATHER lingering in the tool aisle.

"How did it go with Bernard?" she asked.

"He's in."

"And he made the phone call?"

"I saw him call Fiona myself."

"And she took the bait?"

He nodded. "Hook, line, and sinker. She sounded eager to get her hands on the 'valuables' Nigella left in her beekeeping shed."

Claire allowed herself a small, satisfied smile.

"Hopefully, she'll take time out of her busy packing schedule to make an appearance. Without her, this plan might not work."

"We might be grasping at straws as it is," he warned her, looking around the empty aisle before adding, "Are you certain Tom is the man we're looking for?"

Claire nodded. "He's got away with poisoning twice already. It's time to force his hand. He thinks he's untouchable, so why not go for a third?"

<hr>

AT TWENTY-FIVE MINUTES PAST TWO, CLAIRE WANDERED into the café. The place was packed with only a few empty tables. One was next to a figure half-hidden behind a newspaper in the corner—glimpses of golden, shiny hair poked over the top.

Instead, she chose a table near the middle of the small

greenhouse, picking up the laminated menu as she sat down. From the corner of her eye, she noticed Bernard manning the counter in a green apron. Perfect. He gave her a cursory nod, which she returned politely before pretending to examine a menu.

Five minutes later, at exactly half-past two, Claire glanced up to see Fiona Turner striding into the café, handbag hooked over one arm, a phone at her ear. Her hair was scraped into a messy bun, many wisps of auburn hair escaping the updo. She was still smartly dressed, but from the few stray strands alone, it was the least put-together Claire had seen her.

"Bernard," Fiona called, tapping her hand on the counter to get his attention. He was scratching his head at the coffee machine like it was his first time seeing it. "These valuables?"

"I'll be with you in a moment, Fiona. Let me finish up this order."

"I don't have time for this," she huffed. "I have a flight to catch, and I need to finish packing."

"Take a seat, and I'll be right with you," he said, not moving from the machine. "I'll make you some tea. I won't be long."

"Fine," she conceded, "but make it green."

Fiona grumbled but sank into the chair at the next table with her back turned to Claire. Taking the menu to the counter, Claire ordered a cup of berry tea. She breezed past Fiona, expecting her to look up, but she was too busy typing something on her phone. Her perfect manicure had chipped, and she didn't have the sweet cloud of perfume encasing her.

Bernard took the cups of tea into the kitchen to steep, and everything was going to plan. That was, until Claire's mother, Janet, barged into the café. Sarah followed her, a little more color in her cheeks than the last time Claire had seen her, but by no means recovered.

"Claire?" Janet cried. "*There* you are!"

This wasn't part of the plan.

"Not now, Mother!"

Sarah and Fiona froze at the sight of each other. Fiona stood up, slinging her bag over her shoulder and set off across the café.

"Claire, dear, Sarah has something important to tell you," Janet said. "She's remembered—"

"In a minute, Mother," Claire whispered, cutting across the café as Fiona neared the door. Plastering on a smile, she stepped in front of her. "Fiona? I thought it was you."

"Do I…" She squinted, looking Claire up and down. The 'mortgage outfit' really must have worked wonders. "Oh, it's *you*. What do you want? I have somewhere to be."

"I just wanted to apologise for the way I've hounded you this past week," Claire forced out, trying her best to look apologetic. "It was none of my business. Curiosity got the better of me, I suppose. Seems we'll never know the truth about what happened to Nigella." She lowered her gaze. "I shouldn't have pried."

Fiona considered her a moment, her reserve cracking. "Yes, well... I appreciate you saying that, but I really must—"

Claire opened her mouth to respond when she noticed Tom slip into the café beside Fiona. Her pulse spiked at the sight of the bulky gloves covering his hands as his fingers closed on Fiona's shoulder.

"You're not bothering my sister again, are you, Claire?"

"She was apologising," Fiona spoke for her. "It's sorted, Tom."

"I should hope so."

"Like I was telling Fiona," Claire continued, somehow maintaining her smile as Tom's eyes narrowed on her. "Curiosity got the better of me."

"What's that old saying?" Tom's brows darted up. "Curiosity killed the cat? Fiona, don't you have packing to finish?"

"Yes, I was just going—"

"*Tea!*" Bernard announced, rounding the counter with a tray. "What table are you sitting at, Fiona? I'll go and fetch those valuables for you."

Fiona glanced at Sarah on the other side of the café, sat next to Janet, who was glaring with pursed lips. Fiona returned to her table and sunk into her chair, followed by Tom, and then Bernard.

Claire took her seat and smiled her thanks as Bernard set the white cup in front of her. Bernard nodded, and without taking a moment to think about it, Claire blew on the surface and took her first sip.

Tom's eyes didn't leave her.

She smiled.

He smiled back.

She took another sip.

He couldn't stop the smile from twisting into a smirk.

Bernard continued to the next table and placed a red cup before Fiona. Claire watched Tom as she licked her lips before going back for more, and Tom was so fixated on watching his plan unfold he didn't notice the red cup until it was at Fiona's lips.

"Oh, Bernard?" Claire called across the café, pointing at her cup. "I think you gave me the wrong one. I ordered berry tea, not green."

"Ah, my mistake," he called back, folding his arms behind the counter with a satisfied grin. "Accidents happen."

Tom's head snapped towards his sister, eyes bulging. As quick as a viper, his gloved hand shot out and knocked Fiona's teacup from her grip. It hit the linoleum floor and shattered, steaming tea splashing across their shoes.

"Tom!" Fiona cried. "Have you lost your mind?"

Tom could only stare at the broken cup, chest heaving. Taking a deep slurp of tea, Claire watched the color drain from Fiona's cheeks as she stared at her brother in wide-eyed disbelief.

"You saved the day, Tom," Claire spoke into the heavy silence. "Wouldn't want your dear sister to drink something poisonous."

Tom attempted an unconvincing laugh. "Poisonous? Don't be ridiculous. There was a bee, that's all."

Ignoring this transparent lie, Claire turned her gaze toward Sarah. "Sarah, would you mind showing everyone your hands, please?"

Sarah held up her palms, the shiny marks of healing sores visible across her skin.

"Foxglove exposure," Claire continued. "It causes quite a nasty rash if handled. You'd have known that, Tom, if you read all of that page in the wildflower book. I suppose you stopped after the 'poisonous when ingested line', right? Mind showing us your hands?"

Tom scowled, clenching his fists. "Why on earth would I go around handling poisonous plants?"

"To make your very own tea blend in handy dandy teabags," Claire said evenly. "Tea, which you slipped into Nigella's afternoon cup and then Sarah's. And today, mine."

She reached into her pocket and pulled out a zip-lock plastic bag containing inconspicuous-looking teabags.

She slapped them on the table of the man holding the newspaper. It rustled, but whatever he was reading was more interesting than what was happening in the café.

"Thanks for letting my good friend, Sally, in this morning for an inspection, Fiona." At this, Fiona made a small, strangled sound, pressing a hand over her mouth. "She's quite the resourceful opportunist when she needs to be, as are you, Tom."

"Shut up," he growled. "You've gone far enough."

"Hardly," she said. "You're broke, aren't you, Tom? Why else would you be living with your sister, begging estate agents to look past your credit... manipulating young women into taking out loans on your behalf." She darted her brows up at him. "You saw an opportunity to expand your sister-in-law's modest honey business— more of a passion project—into a lucrative empire. But she refused to exploit her bees that way. Nigella wouldn't be manipulated, not even by her wife, to save her ill-matched marriage."

Fiona flinched at this.

"Nigella knew who she was, and what she stood for," Claire pressed on. "So, you concocted your deadly plan to replace her with a more malleable queen." She tipped her head towards the doorway. Hayley lingered at the front of a crowd gathering to watch what was unfolding. "You had no idea how to manage the colony, did you? You didn't care about them, only what they could do for you.

Nigella taught Hayley everything she knew, and that's all you needed."

"Lies!" Tom burst out, face mottled purple now. "Prove it!"

"Gladly." Claire turned to Sarah once more. "Sarah, my mother said you remembered something. From the day you came to be interviewed to get your job back, I presume?"

The timid girl nodded, looking nervously at Tom. "I —I went to say goodbye to the hives. To Nigella, really. I didn't think I'd be coming back here, and that's when I saw Tom. That's when I noticed the rash on his hands." She paused, swallowing hard before lifting her chin with quiet defiance. "I should've told the police right away. But I thought there might be an honest explanation. I knew what it felt like to be wrongly accused."

"And you thanked her by poisoning her!" Janet cried. "She has children. Have you no shame?"

"You were stealing from Nigella," Hayley spoke up, and Claire's father had joined her in the doorway. "It *was* you I saw that day, filling those bags with Nigella's equipment."

"And my tool stock," Bernard growled from the counter. "You took my keys."

"And you were the one who vandalised my shed... twice!" Alan added, shaking his head. "And left those threatening jars to threaten my daughter and I not to come to this very conclusion."

Claire folded her arms, regarding Tom coolly. His broad shoulders were hunched, gloved hands fidgeting with a napkin as he avoided her gaze. The incriminating cup of tainted tea sat still on the floor.

"Why did you do it, Tom?" Claire asked. "Why did you murder Nigella?"

Tom scowled, but finally said, "She was foolish, ignoring what was right in front of her. She had a wife ready to start a family, a passion, a successful garden centre begging to stock her premium products for a fair price... and all she had to do was make some small adjustments. But she wouldn't budge or bend for anyone."

"So, you decided to get rid of her," Claire said bluntly. "To take what was hers to twist it to fit your vision."

"I did what I had to do to survive. I could have taken this brand national!"

Claire sighed. "Nigella didn't care about having a honey empire, Tom. From the sounds of it, she had a difficult childhood, forced to grow up too soon. All she wanted was a simple, quiet life with Fiona, caring for her bees, and mentoring Hayley, to pass on her joy and knowledge to someone who would appreciate it. If only she'd known she was training her replacement."

She glanced at Hayley standing in the doorway, and they shared a small smile.

"My business plans were perfect," Tom burst out angrily. "She was wasting her potential. She had a route to market on her doorstep."

Claire shook her head. "Then you didn't understand her at all. You saw the bees as a means to an end. Profit and expansion. The less Nigella was willing to bend to your plans, the harder you all pushed," Claire continued, scanning the room. "Bernard, raising the rent when things didn't go your way. Fiona, giving ultimatums to make her abandon a part of herself to live your version of life. And you, Tom, slipping foxglove into her tea so you could steam ahead without her."

"You're evil," Sarah muttered from the back of the café. "Nigella was one of the good ones."

Tom rolled his eyes. "Oh, please. I could have let Nigella blame you for those thefts, but I didn't."

"Keeping Sarah around benefited you," Alan spoke up, stepping into the café. "It muddied the waters and distracted from the truth, casting light on another suspect."

"You may have fooled some people, Tom." Claire leaned forward, meeting his eyes directly. "But the truth has a way of flying free eventually. Ramsbottom? I assume you've heard enough?"

The man in the corner slapped his newspaper down

to reveal the detective inspector. He straightened his tie before picking up the plastic bag containing the teabags. "Terrible, terrible business. Now, officers, what are you waiting for? You heard his confession. Arrest this man."

Half of the café stood up at once.

Claire had known DI Ramsbottom was behind the paper from his toupee, but she hadn't realised she'd had such a vast official audience.

Tom weaved through the plain-clothed officers, first for the crowd in the doorway. Hayley and Alan stepped forward, diverting him to the counter. Like he had at the gate, when he'd had his hands concealed in his hoodie pocket, Tom hopped over the counter. Bernard was waiting for him, and so was his clenched fist. Blood spurted from his nose as he spun around and creased over the counter. Shaking his hand out, Bernard looked down with a satisfied nod as the officers cuffed Tom's hands behind his back. Ramsbottom dragged off the gardening gloves to reveal thick red rashes that put Sarah and Sally's to shame.

Every time Claire had seen him, they'd been covered. The beekeeping suits, the gardening gloves, his hoodie pockets, the shaving foam…

"Don't let her leave!" Tom cried. "She's just as guilty!"

They turned to see Fiona attempting to slip quietly through the crowd. She froze like a deer in headlights as the wall of onlookers solidified.

"What's he talking about?" Ramsbottom cried.

When she didn't respond, Tom sneered. "Go on then, tell them. Tell them how you asked me to get rid of Nigella to make your fresh start run smoother. Tell them how you didn't want to split a penny of your assets with her."

"I—I didn't mean *murder*, Tom!" Fiona said through gritted teeth.

"Oh, so you left out that book about poisonous plants with the page turned over for what reason?" His smirk spread again. "You promised me a share of what you didn't want to give Nigella if I cleared the path, but you were never going to pay up, were you?"

"You..." Fiona's lips dragged into a snarl as officers pulled her hands behind her back. "You couldn't have just let me get away, could you? I deserved a fresh start."

"Why?" Claire asked flatly. "That's the one thing Nigella will never get now."

Fiona's haughty mask crumbled completely. Tears shone in her eyes, but Claire steeled herself against feeling any sympathy for her. She watched silently as DI Ramsbottom led the siblings away, Tom still spewing vitriol while Fiona stared ahead with a numb glare.

Claire sagged into her chair with a deep exhale. She tossed back the last of the green tea. Vile. She'd stick to coffee. But it was over at last. Nigella might have been denied her fresh start, but at least Fiona and Tom's would take place behind bars.

"Well done, little one," her father said, patting her on the back. "Couldn't have put any of that better myself."

LATER THAT AFTERNOON, CLAIRE MADE HER WAY TO THE hives, where Hayley was moving bees into temporary boxes. The young woman's eyes were red-raw, but she had a resolute steel in her stare as she worked.

At Claire's approach, she swiped the back of her hand across her cheeks.

"I should never have trusted him." She gave a watery, self-deprecating laugh. "Some apprentice I turned out to be. Nigella wouldn't have fallen for what I did. She'd have read the loan contracts—it would never have gone that far."

Claire's heart ached for her. She hugged Hayley tight, feeling her thin frame tremble with suppressed sobs.

"Don't be so hard on yourself," she murmured. "How old are you?"

"Twenty-one."

"Perfect age for making mistakes." She pulled back, brushing the girl's frizzing braid over her shoulder. "Trust me, I racked up credit card debt like mad when I was your age. Felt too much like free money."

Hayley gave a teary chuckle.

"Really?"

"Only finished paying them off last year," Claire said with a wink. "What will you do now? With the hives?"

"I'm going to take them far away from Meadowview." She stiffened up, casting a glance at the glass building. "Bernard offered to lower the rent, but it's too much pressure. My gran has a beautiful garden out in the countryside. They can have a fresh start there without the pressure to pay rent."

"That's a lovely idea. Nigella would approve, I'm sure."

They shared a smile before Hayley pulled her in for another impulsive hug. "Thank you, Claire," she whispered. "I really did fall for everything he said. He was quite charming when nobody else was around. I can already feel the smoke clearing."

Inside Meadowview Garden Centre, a celebratory mood filled the air. Claire, her father, and DI Ramsbottom chatted near the entrance, soaking in the afternoon sunshine streaming through the glass walls.

"Well done again, Alan," Ramsbottom said, slapping him on the back. "Another murder case tidied up."

"Oh, I can't take much credit this time around. Claire's the one who connected all the dots and set the trap. She would make a fine detective."

Claire grinned at the praise. "Only because I had your wisdom to draw from, Dad."

"Nonsense. You've got sharp instincts—better than mine ever were. Watching you piece together the truth about Tom made me so proud."

Claire's heart swelled. It had been a trying few weeks, but now, with the warm spring sun on her face and her father's pride wrapping around her, she felt nothing but deep contentment.

Justice had been served.

Nigella could rest peacefully now.

And her legacy was in good hands with Hayley.

Bernard walked over from the café, still in the apron, balancing a tray laden with cakes and biscuits.

"Thought you all deserved a treat after everything," he offered. "Please, help yourselves."

Ramsbottom's eyes lit up. "Don't mind if I do."

As the men ate, Bernard turned to Alan. "I... I wanted to apologise for how I acted at your house yesterday. I was out of sorts, but that's no excuse." He looked down, abashed. "I can't help but see the part I planned in Tom's sick plan with how I treated Nigella. I promise things will be different around here from now on. I'd be honoured if you wanted your old job back, Alan."

Alan considered the offer as he chewed through a chocolate bourbon. When he finally spoke, it was slowly and deliberately. "That's decent of you, Bernard. I did enjoy the work. But this murder business has made me realise retirement suits me just fine. I appreciate the offer, truly, but I believe it's time for me to get back to tending my garden." He gave the man a kind smile. "Though I would suggest removing the foxgloves from your stock. And treating your staff, café waiters included, better in the future."

Bernard nodded as his gaze drifted to where Sarah lingered near the café entrance. Setting down his tray, he made his way over.

Claire tensed, moving to intervene, but her mother beat her to it. Janet swooped in and steered Sarah away, casting a warning glare at Bernard.

"Oh no, you don't!" Janet said with pursed lips. "You had your chance with this young lady. I've already offered Sarah a position with my cleaning business at double your stingy wages. She's a Janet's Angel now." She gave Sarah's arm a supportive pat. "You'll be able to live comfortably and provide for those children without any extra-curricular activities."

"Mrs Harris, I can't tell you what this means..."

"Please, Janet will do."

Satisfied, Janet returned to Claire and Alan, leaving a humbled Bernard to slink away empty-handed.

"Well, I think that wraps everything up nicely then," Ramsbottom announced, brushing cake crumbs from his suit. "Northash—and all the cups of tea within it—owe you both a debt of gratitude."

"We're just glad it's over," Alan admitted. "No more

mysterious jars of honey or threatening notes to worry about. What an odd case this turned out to be."

"Indeed. You've earned a nice long rest after this one." Ramsbottom clapped them each on the back before strolling for the exit.

With the detective gone, Claire turned to her father.

"I still can't believe Tom was behind it all," she murmured, recalling the past week's events. "To kill his sister-in-law…"

"Desperate men take desperate measures when they have nowhere left to turn. I've seen it often enough before. His willingness to drag his sister down with him at the end says all you need to know."

"Yes, well, it's over now," Janet exclaimed, brushing past them through Meadowview Garden Centre's sliding front doors. "And Alan, do find somewhere else to buy your plants, won't you? I don't think I ever want to come here again."

As they drove away, Claire gave the garden centre one last glance in the rear-view mirror. She'd been right about there being something strange going on at the place, but she wished she hadn't been. They rounded the corner, and like her mother, Claire would be more than happy to never visit again.

CHAPTER SEVENTEEN

*O*ver a week had passed since the arrest of Tom and Fiona, and a sense of peace had returned to the village of Northash. For Claire Harris, life was gradually getting back to normal. On Saturday morning, she awoke early as rays of morning sun streamed in through the window of her flat above the candle shop. After getting dressed, she headed downstairs and began her usual routine of tidying up and preparing for the day ahead.

When she opened the door, however, her heart sank.

Another jar of honey was on her doorstep.

Another written message.

She looked around the square for signs that Tom and Fiona had somehow escaped their cells, but all was quiet in Northash. She picked it up and examined the label, and relief washed over her.

The jar had a new logo. 'Hayley's Honey' scrawled the shiny label in an elegant cursive font, with the words 'In loving memory of the eternal queen bee, Nigella' in smaller print underneath. Claire squinted across the village square and spotted Hayley outside the gym, talking with Em. She waved to the two women, toasting the jar in thanks.

She flipped the tag over: 'Now with no added water!'

Claire laughed as she turned the jar, the honey as thick and golden as Nigella's.

Ten minutes later, Damon arrived, looking a little worse for wear.

"Karaoke or video games?" she asked.

"Neither," he said. "*Doctor Who* marathon."

"Shocker," she said sarcastically.

"It was Sally's idea."

"Okay, that *is* a shocker." She laughed. "It must be love."

As the coffee machine ground the beans for their first cups of the day, Claire explained her intention to take down the wildflower candle display now they'd officially run out of the second batch. She'd considered making more with Hayley's wax offer, but the cloying floral scent carried too many unpleasant memories. She was happy for it to be the shop's first true limited-edition. Besides, summer was knocking at the door, and she had a table full of the perfect new scent, almost cured and ready for labels.

"These are going to sell out. Just you watch," Damon said, inhaling from the open jars. "Ice cream and milkshakes. Genius." He cleared his throat. "What did the newspaper say to the ice cream?"

"If this is another pun…"

"'What's the scoop?'" He elbowed her in the side. "Get it?"

Claire laughed, though she couldn't decide if it was the best or worst joke she'd ever heard. "I'll give you that one, but if you start telling me you've learned countless random facts from *Ice Cream Parlour Simulator 9*, I will fire you."

"Don't be absurd," he said. "They didn't make *nine* of them."

Soon, they were hard at work clearing out the window display. As Claire lifted down the hanging dried flowers and peeled off the bee stickers, she felt a sense of closure.

The little bell above the door tinkled merrily, heralding new arrivals. Claire looked over her shoulder and smiled to see Ryan enter with his children, Amelia and Hugo.

"Can we speak to the manager?" Ryan asked with a knowing grin. "My daughter has a complaint to make."

"You're speaking with her."

"I want 10% of sales for this new candle," Amelia said in a matter-of-fact voice. "You'd never have had the idea if my nagging about ice cream and milkshakes hadn't inspired you."

Claire raised an eyebrow, struggling to keep a straight face. "Hmm, is that so? Well, I'm afraid 10% won't be possible, but how about I pay you back with those milkshakes and ice cream I promised, and as many of the new candles as you want?"

Amelia considered this with a seriousness beyond her years before nodding decisively. "Deal."

"What happened to negotiating?" Hugo asked.

"She said as many as I want," Amelia said, grabbing a basket and heading to the new display of just-labelled jars. "I'll make a fortune selling them on at school."

"Amelia…" Ryan warned.

"Joking, Dad," she said, rolling her eyes as she grabbed a measly two. "Old people…"

In the back room, Claire whizzed chocolate ice cream with milk in a blender, and soon, the kids were enjoying their treats while pitching in to help with the redecorating.

The new ice cream shop theme came together beautifully as the morning wore on. When she finished hanging up the last of the paper bunting and Damon and Ryan had attached the floating giant cardboard cones in the window, the shop felt bright and cheerful, precisely the atmosphere Claire wanted to create after the dark weeks the village had faced.

Claire took a deep breath, consuming the sweet scent of sugary vanilla filling the shop. She was more than ready to take on whatever their fresh start threw at her.

"Ugh. I just got a text message from Sally." Damon winced. "Anyone fancy karaoke tonight?"

———

LATER AT THE HESKETH ARMS, CLAIRE CLENCHED HER eyes as Eugene belted out a painfully off-key rendition of 'Total Eclipse of the Heart' on the makeshift stage. At the next table, Janet was harassing a waiter about putting too much gin in her gin and tonic.

Finally, it was Ryan and Claire's turn at the mic. They cringed at each other as the opening notes of 'Islands in the Stream' played. Claire jumped in on the first verse, matching Ryan's smooth baritone. They swayed together, trying their best to harmonize, spurred on by two pints of homebrew each.

Once they were finished, the small crowd applauded, and they returned to their booth. Flushed with excitement, Ryan turned to Claire and said, "So, I have some news."

"Spit it out."

"Dad got the promotion at the gym!" Amelia announced for him.

"Seriously?"

"Apparently, the owner thought I made some valid points when I staked my claim to the job," he revealed, blushing as his finger circled his pint glass. "Starting next week, I'll be able to set my own hours."

"That's amazing news." Claire threw her arms around him. "I'm so chuffed for you, Ryan."

Over his shoulder, she noticed her parents heading up for their karaoke selection.

"Remember this one, Alan?" Janet trilled as 'Summer Nights' from Grease began playing. To Claire's astonishment, her mother launched into a rather animated rendition of Sandy's part while her father crooned Danny's lines. Their cheeky performance earned hoots and hollers from the inebriated audience, and they finished with deep bows.

"Now, to business," Eugene announced as he stood up on wobbly legs, raising his glass between songs. "A toast to our very own super sleuth, Claire! Without her, the dastardly poisoner might still be roaming free."

Claire flushed, touched by the recognition. She returned the toast, then lifted her drink again. "And to my brilliant father, the best detective partner I could ask for."

Alan beamed and returned the salute. "And to DI

Ramsbottom. The case wouldn't be complete without him sweeping in to take all the credit."

Everyone laughed. Then Janet stood up imperiously, glass in hand. "Yes, yes, you're all splendid. But most importantly, a toast to me for... well, just because."

Janet took a swig amidst affectionate chuckles, and Claire wondered how much the bartender had over-poured the gin.

The karaoke continued, but she tuned out the noise—even as Damon gave his best Cher impression for a comeback with Sally as Sonny—her attention was only on Ryan beside her. He slipped his arm around her waist, eyes twinkling.

"So, duet partners for life?" he asked.

"Always," she whispered, leaning in to kiss him softly. "That's if you can stay on key next time."

"I think you'll find my pitch was perfect."

"You were both rubbish," Amelia said, sticking out her tongue. "C'mon, Hugo. Let's show them how it's done with some 'Baby Shark.'"

Groaning, Hugo reluctantly put down his console and let Amelia drag him across the small dance floor, where Claire's parents were spinning around slowly while someone gave their best slurred Elvis impression.

"You know, if we end up like your parents one day, I'll be happy."

"Yeah, me too," Claire said, resting her head on his shoulder. "I'll try not to turn too much into my mother."

"Our future house would be spotless," he said.

"*Our* future house?"

"Well, you didn't think I was imagining that big house with the garden and treehouse without you, did I?" he said, pulling her in close. "Even if we don't get there and we end up somewhere else, I don't see my life with anyone else, Claire. You, me, and the kids. I thought that was obvious by now."

They kissed, a promise of a bright future together.

With the mystery solved after Tom and Fiona's café confessions, Claire looked forward to life returning to normal. Her candle shop was back in order, Hayley's new honey business was underway, and her family was beside her. And though 'normal' was never exactly boring in Northash, she was ready to enjoy the calm summer days ahead. Maybe they'd even dig out her dad's old camera to make some home videos for the collection. Claire was certain these were days she'd want to look back on in her retirement years.

But for now, Claire was glad to live in the moment. It was Amelia and Hugo's turn for karaoke, and they needed their two biggest cheerleaders on the dance floor.

Thank you for reading, and don't forget to
RATE/REVIEW!

The Claire's Candles story continues in...

FROSTED PLUM FEARS
COMING DECEMBER 19th! PRE-ORDER NOW!

**Sign up to Agatha's mailing list at AgathaFrost.com
and don't miss an update...**

WANT TO BE KEPT UP TO DATE WITH AGATHA FROST RELEASES? *SIGN UP THE FREE NEWSLETTER!*

www.AgathaFrost.com

You can also follow **Agatha Frost** across social media. Search 'Agatha Frost' on:

Facebook
Twitter
Goodreads
Instagram

ALSO BY AGATHA FROST

Claire's Candles

1. Vanilla Bean Vengeance

2. Black Cherry Betrayal

3. Coconut Milk Casualty

4. Rose Petal Revenge

5. Fresh Linen Fraud

6. Toffee Apple Torment

7. Candy Cane Conspiracies

Peridale Cafe

1. Pancakes and Corpses

2. Lemonade and Lies

3. Doughnuts and Deception

4. Chocolate Cake and Chaos

5. Shortbread and Sorrow

6. Espresso and Evil

7. Macarons and Mayhem

8. Fruit Cake and Fear

9. Birthday Cake and Bodies

10. Gingerbread and Ghosts

Other

Printed in Great Britain
by Amazon